Marquis For Marianne

Blushing Brides
Book 2

Catherine Bilson

ISBN: 0-6481743-6-3

ISBN-13: 978-0-6481743-6-3

Other Books by Catherine Bilson

The Best Of Relations

Infamous Relations

Mr Bingley's Bride

A Christmas Miracle At Longbourn

An Earl For Ellen

A Duke For Diana (forthcoming)

For information on forthcoming works as well as free short reads, visit my website at:

www.catherinebilson.com

Contents

Chapter One

A Private Ball at Temple Grove Manor, near Cambridge
March, 1810

"Your most persistent suitor is back, Miss Abingdon."

Marianne permitted only a slight smile to touch her lips as Amelia Temple spoke. The other girl's tone held just the slightest hint of jealousy, as the tall young man approaching the pair was easily the handsomest in the room -- especially in a lieutenant's scarlet regimentals.

"I've been acquainted with Mr. Rotherhithe since we were both children, Miss Temple," Marianne attempted to defray Amelia's envy. "We are friends; that is all." The lie almost scalded her tongue, but it would not do for whispers of her true attachment to Alexander Rotherhithe to reach her father's ears. Or, God forbid, *his* father's or grandfather's ears.

"Miss Abingdon." Alexander bowed very correctly, his dark brown eyes warm as he straightened to gaze upon her face. "Dare I hope you have a space remaining on your dance card for me?"

Without a word, Marianne slipped the ribbon holding the tiny booklet from about her wrist and offered it to him. His lips quirked minutely as he examined the card before lifting the equally tiny pencil attached and jotted his initials down in the single space remaining. She had saved that precious space by dint of avoiding as many potential dance partners as possible, no easy feat when you were lauded as the greatest beauty of the Season.

"I shall consider myself exceptionally fortunate, Miss Abingdon. Until our dance, then." He bowed once again and left them alone.

Amelia sighed wistfully as she watched the lieutenant depart and muttered, "I wish he'd asked *me* to dance."

"Since your card is full already, it would do you no good if he had," Marianne pointed out dryly.

"As the daughter of the house, your dances have all been reserved since the house party began!"

"True, but still, he could have asked," Amelia sighed again before linking her arm through Marianne's. "I hear the orchestra tuning up. We should go into the ballroom; the first set will begin shortly."

Marianne did not care in the slightest for the first set, or any set other than the one she would dance with Alexander. Nevertheless, she painted a false smile on her lips and allowed herself to be led onto the floor.

He hated every man who dared approach her.

She was his, had always been his. Ever since he'd laid eyes on her years ago, her auburn-haired perfection had drawn him like a moth to a flame. Every other girl paled into boring insignificance beside her spectacular, eye-catching beauty.

She was too young then, of course, but now she was a woman grown. Eighteen years old and ripe for the plucking, a peach just ready to drop into his waiting hand. Especially considering her father, who was even now gambling away the last of his late wife's money at the gaming tables.

Taking a sip of his brandy, he watched with narrowed eyes as a tall young sprig in a scarlet coat claimed her hand for a dance. How dare that upstart touch what was his!

Soon, nobody would be allowed to dance with her but him.

Very soon.

"It's terribly warm in here," Marianne said as the musicians struck the first chords. "Would you mind terribly if we sat out the dance? I think perhaps I should get some air."

"Of course," Alexander said with a secret little smile, promptly escorting her from the floor. "I would not for a moment have you distress yourself for the sake of a mere dance, Miss Abingdon. Pray, retire to refresh yourself."

"Thank you for your understanding, Lieutenant." Marianne curtseyed gracefully before making her way out of the room.

Once out of the ballroom, she did not turn left to ascend the stairs to the retiring rooms. Instead, she turned to the right and opened a door mostly concealed behind a large potted plant, a door which led to the servants' quarters. Lifting her skirts in her hands, she rushed along the narrow, poorly lit corridor as fast as she could in her dancing slippers, hoping desperately nobody was coming the other way. She was lucky, though, and reached her next destination without seeing another soul.

A second door let out below the terrace immediately outside the ballroom, and she stepped out onto the raked gravel, careful not to let her feet make a sound. Directly above her head she could hear voices, people talking and laughing, cigar smoke drifting upwards as some gentleman indulged in the cool night air.

A hand curled around her elbow, and she bit back a gasp. Relaxing at once, she followed the insistent tug of that strong hand, tiptoeing on the loud gravel until they were around the side of the house and walking on grass, moving further away from the lighted windows and the noise until everything became dark and quiet.

"Marianne," he said her name gruffly once they were free to speak without fear of being overheard.

She sobbed his name in return, throwing herself against him. "Oh, Alexander! You came!"

"Nothing could have kept me away." He caught her in strong arms, bending down to kiss her upturned lips.

"Not even your grandfather?" Marianne whispered when he broke the kiss.

13

"It turns out that joining the army has had a remarkably freeing effect. My commanding officer is a great deal less strict than dear Grandpapa."

She could not see his wry smile in the darkness, but she could hear it in his voice. Smiling herself, she rested her head against his chest, heedless to the disarray of her curls. His warm hand came up to rest at the back of her neck and for a long moment they remained thus, in a close and loving embrace.

"I wish I could ask you to come away with me now," Alexander murmured, "but my regiment is bound for Spain next week. Even if we were to marry, I have no safe haven to provide you."

"It doesn't matter," Marianne said fiercely. "Just promise me you'll be careful, Alex? Promise you'll come back to me?"

They both knew there were no guarantees in war. Both of them had lost family and friends to the war against the French: Marianne, her only brother; Alexander, two uncles and his best friend from his school days.

Still, Alexander promised her, and he meant every word. "If God grants that I survive, I will come back to you, Marianne. There is no force on earth which will stop me coming for you, if you will but wait for me."

His words had the solemnity of a marriage vow, and in his mind they were exactly that. In that moment, he pledged himself to the girl who he had known all his life. The girl who had been his childhood companion in numerous escapades. The girl who had been his shoulder to cry on when his baby sister died of fever, just as he had returned the favour a year later when her mother drowned in a tragic accident. The girl who he loved above all others. And always would.

"I will wait for you," Marianne pledged in return, reaching up to place her hands on his cheeks, and though he could not see her eyes, in his mind they glowed blue as the summer sky, bright with her love. "I will *always* wait for you."

He watched the young officer return to the ballroom from the terrace, his smile a great deal too self-satisfied for a man who'd lost out on dancing with the most beautiful girl at the ball. Moments later, Marianne walked back in through the main doors, smiling just as happily.

Two pairs of eyes met and secret glances were exchanged before both looked away, feigning gaiety while mingling with the other partygoers.
He downed the last of his brandy.
It was time to make his move.

Chapter Two

*The townhouse of the Earl of Havers, London
November, 1818*

"He's dead."

Marianne stared in disbelief.

"Lady Creighton?"

Behind her, the whispers began: *"Poor
thing." "She's in shock." "So sudden."*

"Lady Creighton, I think you'd best sit
down."

A strong hand touched her elbow, guided her
away from her husband's body. Out of the room
entirely, to a smaller, empty parlour and a couch
where she was pressed to sit down.

"Marianne," her friend Ellen said, taking a
seat beside her, looking and sounding desperately

concerned. "Are you all right? Please, say something. Should we fetch a doctor?"

"I think it's rather too late for that," Marianne said and then had to suppress a totally inappropriate giggle. "My husband is dead."

"Thomas," Ellen said, and her husband of less than a day immediately moved to her side. "A drink, do you think?"

"Brandy," the Earl of Havers agreed. Within moments he knelt by the couch, pressing a glass into Marianne's hand, which she only then realised was shaking. "Drink it, Lady Creighton. You've had a terrible shock."

"I'm so sorry," she said. "At your wedding party..."

"Don't you dare apologise!" Ellen almost pushed the glass to her lips, forcing her to take a sip. The brandy burned all the way down her throat.

"Lady Creighton," Thomas said, and she couldn't stop her flinch. He paused and began again, "Forgive me for being familiar - Marianne. Will you allow me to handle things regarding the disposition of your husb- I mean, Lord Creighton's body? I assume he should be returned to his estate?"

"Yes."

She should say more, Marianne realised when the pair of them just stared at her. Thomas was an

American, only lately come to England when he'd inherited his title. Though Ellen was possibly the only person she could truly call a friend, her friend was the daughter of a country parson, with no knowledge of society.

"It's near Durham," she managed to get out. "I - perhaps Lord Creighton's valet would be able to give you some useful information."

"Yes," Thomas agreed with some relief. "Yes, of course. I'm sure he will. I'll get right to it, then." He exchanged a glance with Ellen which somehow conveyed a great deal, before leaving the room and closing the door behind him with a soft click.

"Drink the rest of this," Ellen said quietly, urging the glass back to Marianne's lips, "and then I'm going to ring for my maid. You remember Susan? She's terribly efficient. We'll get you up to your room and then you can rest. You've had a terrible shock."

Yes, Marianne thought, letting Ellen coax her into drinking the rest of the brandy. *It is indeed shocking when your husband suffers an apoplectic fit while reproaching you for smiling at the man your friend married just yesterday, dropping dead at your feet.*

She must keep herself together, lest Ellen think she had run mad. So she called upon years of training, years of controlling even her slightest expression, to rein her emotions in. It was not until hours later, when she had finally convinced Ellen and her terrifyingly efficient maid that she was perfectly fine and only wished to be alone, that she could finally allow her feelings to show.

Standing at the window of her bedroom, in the magnificent suite she had been allotted as one of the guests of honour at Ellen's wedding, she watched as the carriage bearing a hastily-procured casket containing her late husband's earthly remains rolled away from the house and down the long avenue of larch trees, bare now of leaves. She would have to follow, of course, and remain at Creighton Hall for the foreseeable future, at least until her period of mourning had ended.

But now, for the first time in more years than she cared to remember, Marianne was *free*.

She had thought she would laugh, in this moment.

The tears surprised her; she had thought there were no more tears left to weep. Years of pain and suffering, loneliness and fear, had dried them all up. Yet the view of the receding carriage blurred, fat drops raced down her cheeks, and Marianne

Creighton fell to her knees and wept in sheer, unadulterated relief.

Chapter Three

Brooks' Gentlemen's Club, London
November, 1819

"You look bored to tears, Glenkellie."

"Give it a few years, Havers." Alexander Rotherhithe, Marquis of Glenkellie, looked up from the news sheet he had been perusing without really taking in any of the information. "Everything in London will bore you to tears, too."

The young Earl of Havers laughed, taking the free seat at Alex's table without waiting to be invited. Which was probably why Alex liked the American; it wasn't so much that he had no idea of the niceties of behaviour, but more that he thought they were utter nonsense and refused to abide by them. The seat was free, and Thomas wanted to sit down. Why wait for Alex to ask, just because he happened to possess a loftier title?

Setting the news sheet down, Alex smiled at Thomas. They had only met a few months ago, when Thomas brought his new wife down to London for the Little Season, but hit it off right away. Alex was tired of sycophants and toadies, of those too intimidated by his wealth and title to want to get to know the real him. Thomas' cheerful disregard for protocol was a breath of fresh air.

"Drink?" Alex suggested, gesturing to an attentive waiter.

"I'll have what you're having." Thomas nodded to his cup on the table.

"Coffee? Sure you wouldn't like anything stronger?"

"I've promised to take Ellen to a ball tonight. If I start in on anything stronger now, I'll not see it through until four, or whatever ridiculous hour these things finish." Thomas grimaced. "I'm looking forward to heading back to Herefordshire and going to bed before midnight, for once!"

Alex had to laugh. "You're such a provincial, Havers."

"Says the man whose estate comprises much of the remotest parts of Scotland," Thomas shot back dryly.

"Why do you think I'm in London? Nothing up there but cranky crofters and sheep. Castle Glenkellie is only tolerable for a month or two in the summer, and barely that. Were it not entailed, I'd sell the lot and live here year-round."

The words were empty, and Thomas' sharp-eyed stare let Alex know he wasn't fooled. The truth was: Alex loved his home no matter the time of year. He simply couldn't bear it when his mother was in residence, as she was at the moment. God willing, she'd take it into their heads to tour Greece or Italy or some such place soon, and he'd be able to go home without fear of her producing a bride for him out of thin air.

Thomas' coffee arrived, and he sat back in his chair, relaxing as he took a sip of the hot, fragrant brew. "Rather you than me," he said, and it took Alex a moment to realise Thomas was talking about living in London. "In fact, we're heading home earlier than we planned. As much as Ellen has enjoyed our visit this time around, she wants to be home in plenty of time for Christmas. In fact, she plans to host a house party, and she has charged me with extending an invitation to you."

Surprised, Alex paused with his own coffee cup an inch or so from his lips. While he had met the lovely young Countess of Havers on several occasions and even stood up with her at a few dances, they'd had little chance to get to know each other. "Why?" he asked bluntly, lowering the cup.

Thomas looked amused. "Because she knows you and I have struck up a friendship, Glenkellie. Ellen has made plenty of friends among the ladies -- both married and single -- and has invited a number of them, but none of their attached husbands, brothers, or fathers are people I would call a close friend. You, on the other hand, are. She asked if I should like to invite you, I said I would, and she wrote out an invitation." Slipping a cream-coloured envelope from his pocket, he placed it on the table between them. "Should you fancy an escape from the delights of London for a few days without journeying to the frozen wastes of the north, we would be delighted to have you."

Touched, nonetheless Alexander affected disinterest as he picked up the envelope, broke the seal, and perused the brief invitation written in the Countess of Havers' own hand. Ellen had been raised a country parson's daughter, and her handwriting bore none of the flourishes and curlicues the daughters of the aristocracy were wont to affect; it was plain, neat, and very readable.

"How kind," Alexander murmured distantly. "Perhaps I will join you for a few days. It might be diverting."

Thomas smirked into his coffee, and Alex knew he hadn't fooled the American in the slightest. The truth was, he'd already received and rejected more than a dozen invitations to Christmas house parties, many of them at homes both more magnificent and more conveniently situated to London than Havers Hall, a good three days' journey away in Herefordshire, near the Welsh border.

All those invitations, however, had been extended by families with marriageable daughters looking to snag a marquis to hang on their family tree. Thomas and Ellen had no such ulterior motive. No, they had invited him quite simply for the pleasure of his company, and therefore he made up his mind then and there to accept the offer.

"Has Lady Havers invited many single ladies?" he asked in a last-ditch effort to talk himself out of it.

"Only a couple, I believe, and they're rather of the bluestocking variety who definitely wouldn't be likely to set their caps for you, never fear. There's also a widowed friend of hers who we hope to persuade to come."

"Ah, merry widows. Those I appreciate." Alex grinned wickedly.

Thomas shook his head, laughing in his good-natured way. "Don't play the rake with me, Glenkellie, I've seen you roll your eyes when ladies of the demi-rep make eyes at you. You've no more interest in them than I do, and have not even the good reason of a wife you adore!"

"You haven't known me all that long, Havers. For the right bird of paradise, I can be very accommodating indeed."

"I don't think Lady Creighton will be falling into your arms, charming as I'm sure you can be if you make the effort," Thomas said dryly.

Alex froze in the act of setting down his coffee cup. "Lady Creighton? The... former countess?"

Thomas' brow wrinkled. "Correct, though I think she's technically still a countess. Ellen says 'Marianne, Lady Creighton' is the correct address now, however. Since she's not the mother of the current earl, she's not a dowager." He looked exasperated. "Have I the right of that, or do I need to consult Debrett's again? I swear, the whole English system of titles and honorifics has the most abstruse rules; it's worse than conjugating Latin verb tenses! Sometimes I think Lady Jersey just makes them up as she goes along."

Alex burst out laughing, entertained as always by Thomas' irreverent wit. "It's quite possible you're correct," he said between guffaws, "but it's almost certainly not the done thing to talk about it!"

Thomas grinned unrepentantly. "Oh, I don't know. I'm sure Lady Jersey would be highly entertained if she found out I'd said it!"

"Only because she likes your wife so much." His chuckles subsiding, Alex picked up his coffee cup and drained the last of it. "Very well, Havers. Please tell Lady Havers I shall be delighted to accept your invitation to spend the Christmas season with you at Havers Hall."

"You can tell her yourself," Thomas said, finishing off his own coffee. "She also told me to invite you to dinner tonight, if you're not otherwise engaged."

"Well, I'd planned to dine here, but the chance to spend an evening being amused by you and charmed by your lovely lady is far too tempting to pass up."

"Excellent, we'll see you around seven, then? I must take my leave, I'm sorry. Tomorrow is our first wedding anniversary and I have to stop by Garrard's to collect Ellen's gift."

"Until this evening, then." Alex nodded in farewell and watched as Thomas collected his hat and coat and left the club, speaking cheerfully to several gentlemen as he passed.

Havers was possibly the most likable man he'd ever met, Alex mused, and he wondered whatever he had done to attract as a friend a man who could befriend literally anyone.

Lifting one hand, he fingered the long, livid scar down his cheek, where a Frenchman's bayonet had nearly skewered him at Waterloo. The tip of the blade had missed his eye by less than a quarter inch, scraping downwards and flaying his cheek to the bone, ripping a long gash all the way to his chin. The infection afterwards had nearly cost Alex his life.

The jagged scar, still red almost four years later, was ugly enough that several young women of less than robust constitutions had been sickened by it. One had even swooned from the horror. He hadn't yet met one who could look him in the eyes and not stare at his scar with a horrified fascination, riveted by its ugliness.

Alexander Rotherhithe was no longer the perfectly handsome young man a diamond of the

Ton had sworn her heart to. The scar pulled as he smiled tightly, hitching one corner of his mouth up into a grimace.

Marianne Abingdon hadn't waited for him as she had promised. She hadn't even done him the courtesy of sending him a letter, telling him she'd chosen another. The first he'd known of her betrayal was when a brother officer had wordlessly handed him a copy of a month-old newspaper, folded open to the announcements of marriages, and the bottom had fallen out of his world.

Alex remembered little of the next few months. He'd drowned his sorrows in liquor, whenever he could find any, and in leading suicidal charges in every damned battle across the Iberian Peninsula. Or so it seemed later, when he'd finally come out of his haze to realise he'd been promoted (twice!) and decorated with more medals and mentions in dispatches than any one soldier should earn in a lifetime of war, never mind only two years of it.

How he'd escaped death; he had no idea. But somehow he had. Because of it he'd drawn around him a cadre of devoted soldiers who had convinced themselves he was some sort of god of war -- unbeatable on the battlefield.

An officer who could inspire that sort of loyalty was far too valuable to the War Office to have anywhere else but on the battlefield. Even during Bonaparte's exile on Elba, Alex hadn't been permitted to return to England. Only when he was finally -- shockingly -- wounded at Waterloo, proving himself mortal after all, was he allowed to leave the field. He recuperated in Brussels, and as soon as he was fit to sit a horse, he was set to be sent straight back out again to mop up stray pockets of French resistance.

Perhaps he'd have carried on fighting England's wars until he grew old and grey or a bullet proved he was only mortal in the most final way possible, but for a freak accident of succession. Once fourth in line to the marquisate, he'd suddenly become the heir apparent when his uncle, cousin and father were all killed in a flood which swept away their hunting party as they descended a narrow gully.

His grandfather had summoned Alex home peremptorily, and not even the lords at the War Office were inclined to deny the old man his only living heir -- no matter how useful a soldier.

Packed onto a ship bound for Inverness with no ceremony at all, Alex had arrived home barely in time to bid farewell to his grandfather. Brokenhearted by the death of both his sons and the grandson he'd raised from birth to be his successor, Duncan Rotherhithe had cast one disparaging look over Alex and declared, "You'll have to do, I suppose," before drawing his final breath.

He'd been living down to his grandfather's expectations ever since.

Chapter Four

Creighton Hall, Cumbria
Early December, 1819

"Another letter for you, Aunt Marianne." Her nephew Arthur, the new Earl of Creighton, passed the letter to her from the stack a footman had just delivered to the breakfast table on a silver salver.

"Thank you," Marianne said sedately, taking the letter and putting it into her pocket.

"You will not read it now?" Her successor as Countess, Lavinia, peered at her from watery blue eyes. *Curiosity sharpens her already thin face, making her look rather like a ferret,* Marianne thought whimsically.

"It is only from my friend Ellen," she disclaimed quietly, lifting her cup to take a sip of

Catherine Bilson

tea. "No doubt full of inane gossip from Herefordshire."

"You do exchange a lot of letters with her," Arthur said peevishly. "The postage costs a pretty penny."

Marianne took a deep, unseen breath to suppress her immediate urge to make a sharp retort. "She is a faithful correspondent," she answered after a moment, "but an excellent contact to maintain, nonetheless. With Lady Diana to make her debut next Season, I feel it is imperative to keep my Society friendships alive."

"Yes," Lavinia said quickly with a sharp glance at her husband, "yes, of course, you must maintain the friendship, Marianne. The Countess of Havers will be an invaluable friend to have when Diana makes her bows, Arthur."

Marianne hid her smile behind her cup as Arthur sighed and acquiesced to Lavinia's demand. The new Earl had been raised on a very limited allowance and still liked to pinch a penny until it squeaked. Without expectation of inheriting the title since his uncle had been most determined to sire an heir, neither Arthur nor Lavinia had ever even been to London. They knew nobody and would be dependent on Marianne to make their

34

introductions when their eldest daughter was presented.

Marianne had no intention of informing them Ellen had far fewer friends among the London set than Marianne herself. With Ellen as her only regular correspondent, she would lie without compunction to keep her friendship alive.

After all, so very much had already been taken from her.

Much later that day, as she walked back to the small cottage grandiosely named the Creighton Estate Dower House, Marianne slipped the letter from her pocket and broke the seal. She had hoped to escape earlier, but Lavinia required her to be available at all times to assist with her five children -- four of whom were daughters who Lavinia desperately wanted to marry well.

Her father died penniless shortly after her marriage, which left her dependent on Arthur and Lavinia. Since she had never had a dowry and her widow's jointure was almost non-existent, Marianne had no choice but to essentially act as an unpaid finishing school teacher to the four girls, teaching them the social graces they had not learned so far. By the time she led them through a reading in French, given each a half-hour piano lesson and a group singing class, helped them with their needlework, and supervised Diana's efforts at pouring tea, it was late afternoon and Marianne was desperate for some time to herself, even if it was only an hour before she must return to take dinner with the family.

Still in the habit of penny-pinching, Arthur saw no reason to employ a cook for Marianne's use when she could perfectly well take meals with them. It was only grudgingly that he permitted a chambermaid to come over from the main house to clean the cottage and lay the fires and a man to spend an hour or so every other day carrying firewood and water.

"You might as well live in the house with us," Arthur had said when he and Lavinia had first moved in with their children. "Take a room with the girls. No sense opening up the Dower House just for you, is there?"

Lavinia had proved a surprising ally when Marianne insisted she needed her own space. Marianne suspected it was because Lavinia liked to escape over to visit her now and then, taking a break from her noisy, demanding family. Lavinia always brought some biscuits and they would share a quiet cup of tea before returning to the chaos of the main house.

Marianne doubted she and Lavinia would ever be friends - it had to be hard on the new Countess, to have a predecessor ten years her junior still hanging around - and Lavinia was certainly not above using Marianne's dependence on them for her own ends. Still, Marianne would not say she was unhappy.

Not as unhappy as she had been, anyway, even if she no longer wore bright, expensive silk gowns and drank champagne at the most exclusive events in London. Now she wore heavy gowns in the black or grey of mourning, despite her official period ending a month past. Since her husband had preferred to reside in London for most of the year, she had nothing else to wear which was suitable for Creighton's cold winters, and with six dozen gowns in her wardrobe already Arthur would not spend another penny on clothing for her.

Perhaps I should try and sell some of my old gowns, Marianne mused, *or exchange them for some plainer, warmer ones.* Certainly she would not need as many as once she had, even when they repaired to London for Diana's Season.

At least then she would see Ellen again, and the thought warmed her. Settling down in her comfortable chair near the fire in her tiny parlour, she unfolded her letter and began to read.

"You look remarkably pleased with yourself, Aunt Marianne," Arthur remarked as soon as she entered the parlour before dinner.

"I have received an invitation to visit my friend, Lady Havers," Marianne said. "I have already advised her of Diana's upcoming debut, and she proposes that I travel to Haverford to visit with her for a couple of weeks over Christmas and then accompany them on to London to rejoin you in time for the start of the Season."

Arthur had been sipping on a glass of wine; he lowered it now and stared at her, his brow furrowing. "Why would you do that?" he asked, apparently genuinely befuddled.

"Visit with Lady Havers?" Confused in turn, Marianne stared back. "She is my friend, Arthur, and I am very much looking forward to seeing her again. Though we would see her in London, of course, I will be much tied up with Diana…"

"No," Arthur shook his head. "I think there has been some misunderstanding, Aunt Marianne. You're not coming to London."

"What?" Marianne blinked, astonished.

Lavinia did not meet Marianne's eyes when she spoke. "You have done us the very great service of writing letters of introduction to everyone we will need to know, but you need not accompany us yourself. Indeed, it would be much better for you to remain here with the other girls, focusing on their education and their futures."

"Better for whom?" Marianne enquired, then nodded as enlightenment dawned. "Ah… for Diana, of course. You do not want me to be a distraction to any potential suitors, I daresay."

"You flatter yourself." Arthur's expression turned puce. "You're a penniless widow. What possible attraction could you have for the sort of gentlemen who would court an earl's daughter?"

"I have never cared for false modesty," Marianne informed him, "so I will merely say that even when I was an earl's wife, there were never any shortage of gentlemen who should have been courting earls' daughters who preferred to seek my company instead. Though I was never permitted to so much as smile in their direction, much less dance with them."

She saw exactly how it was, and in truth, she could not blame Arthur and Lavinia. Diana was a pretty enough girl and pleasant-natured in a quiet way, but in a room with Marianne she would pale into the background, and they all knew it.

"Very well," Marianne said after a few moments of taut silence. "If I am not to join you in London, so be it. May I at least visit with my friend beforehand and return here when they depart for London?"

"No," Arthur said, and she knew he would not be moved. He stared at her, his lips thinned. "I will not permit it."

"How fortunate, then, that you are not my husband, or my father or brother, and therefore are not in a position of authority to permit or deny me anything!" Marianne's temper flared. She had thought she was done with being controlled by men when Creighton died. She would not tolerate it from a man not even related to her by blood!

"Perhaps not." Arthur's smile was unpleasant. "But I will certainly not permit your use of *our* carriage to travel, and as for money…"

"Arthur," Lavinia said quietly. "Enough."

It's probably a good thing Lavinia stepped in, Marianne thought as she turned and stormed from the parlour, her fists clenched at her sides. *If Arthur had said one more word about my complete lack of funds, I would have slapped him, and goodness knows where that would have ended.*

In the hallway, she almost collided with Diana and her next-in-age sister Clarissa, who both jumped out of her way with startled gasps. She did not even stop to acknowledge them, striding straight back out through the side door she always used and down the short path to her cottage.

I've traded in one prison for another, she thought, stamping her feet as she strode back and forth in her small bedroom. She was still not free to live her life as she chose, and she very likely never would be.

By the following morning, her stomach was grumbling, but Marianne could not bring herself to go up to the house for breakfast and pretend nothing had happened the night prior. She had spent a sleepless night tossing and turning, trying to find a way out of her dilemma and failing. It all came down to money: something of which she had none and no way to get any.

Even if she could find a position as a paid governess or companion, that would be better than working for free for Arthur and Lavinia. But who would hire her? It wasn't as though she had any references. While there might be some rich merchant families who would hire her for the sheer novelty of having a countess work for them, she shied away from the notion. How would she even go about finding such a position, anyway? She had not the faintest idea how such things were done.

A knock at the front door surprised her, and she sighed and went to answer it. She had few visitors, and Lavinia never knocked.

It was a surprise to find Diana and Clarissa on the doorstep, both looking at her with worried eyes. Clarissa held out a small package wrapped in a linen napkin. "Good morning, Aunt Marianne. We - we thought you might be hungry."

She was not too proud, Marianne discovered, to accept the offering. Inside there was a half loaf of fresh bread, a chunk of cheese, and several slices of ham. "Thank you," she managed past a lump in her throat. "That's very kind of you, girls. Would you like to come in?"

Neither of the girls had ever been inside the cottage, and they stepped in shyly, looking about with wide eyes. She gestured them into her tiny parlour, and they sat down together on the little couch, shoulders almost touching.

"Will you excuse me a moment?" She didn't wait for their acquiescence before heading for the kitchen.

When she returned after gulping down a few mouthfuls of the bread, a chunk of cheese, and a slice of ham, she felt a great deal more composed. Taking her usual chair by the fire, she considered the sisters.

There was only a little more than a year between the two girls in age, Marianne knew, and they were very close. Clarissa had more than once expressed distress over Diana's going to London for the upcoming Season, but Marianne had always assumed -- incorrectly, she now realised -- the whole family would be going. Clarissa being left behind would be upsetting for both girls, and not helpful for Diana's nerves at all.

"Thank you for bringing me something to eat," Marianne said finally when neither of the girls seemed inclined to break the silence. "I appreciate your thoughtfulness."

Diana looked at Clarissa, and it was the younger of the sisters who spoke. "I want to go to London too, Aunt Marianne."

"Of course you do," Marianne said understandingly, "but I do not see what you think I can do about it." Clarissa and Dana must have heard everything last night when they listened in the hallway as Arthur humiliated Marianne. It must be obvious to her exactly how little influence Marianne had.

"If you weren't here, Mama and Papa would have to take us all." Diana leaned forward. "If you went to visit Lady Havers, and then joined us in London. Or maybe stayed with the Havers there and just met up with us sometimes."

"I know you both overheard the scene last night, Diana, so you already know it's not a possibility."

"What if you had the money to go, though?" Diana took something from the pocket of her dress. "We both think Papa is very mean to you, and after last night, it's obvious he just wants to keep you here to be, well, a governess, and he's too much of a skinflint even to pay you."

Marianne bit her lip. She would not speak ill of Arthur to his daughters, but it seemed they saw him quite clearly all the same.

"Mama is generous with our allowance, however, and we are not in the habit of spending it. I told Papa this morning I wanted to go to Durham tomorrow and purchase some trinkets before we go to London, and he said we could take the carriage and even gave me some more money." Diana extended the purse she held. "It's not nearly as much as you should have been paid, but we think it should be enough to buy tickets on stagecoaches and rooms at inns to sleep in along the way to Herefordshire"

Marianne hesitated. "Whose idea was this?"

"Mine," Clarissa said firmly. Though she was the younger of the two, she was definitely the leader. "But we are both in agreement this is the right thing to do."

Diana nodded in agreement and tried to press the purse into Marianne's hand. "Please take it. Papa will not think twice of your accompanying us to Durham tomorrow to go shopping, and though you cannot take more than one bag…"

"I could not carry more than one anyway." Coming to a decision, Marianne accepted the purse. "Thank you," she said sincerely. "Come with me, if you will?"

Diana and Clarissa followed her up the narrow stairs to her bedroom and the second, smaller room beyond it which was meant for a maid. Without a maid of her own, however, Marianne used it for her wardrobe - all the beautiful dresses she no longer had occasion to wear were stored there.

"Oh," Diana whispered, amazement on her face as she gazed at the colourful spectacle before her. "Oh, how spectacular!"

"Most of these are not suitable for a debutante, I'm afraid," Marianne said regretfully, brushing her fingers over a wine-red silk gown with a gold lace overdress. "However, there are a few here in lighter colours, and you are very much the same size as me, Diana. They would require minimal alterations for you to wear." Moving confidently among the hanging gowns, she selected one in palest rose, another in spring green with a tiny pink silk flower print, and a silver satin gown which she had never cared for but would look stunning with Diana's dark brown hair and eyes.

"Here," she heaped them into Diana's arms before opening drawers in a dresser and gesturing to Clarissa. "You are not out yet, so I'm afraid none of the gowns would be suitable for you, but there are ribbons and lace aplenty here. Take whatever you wish; it is yours."

"We can't take your lovely things, Aunt Marianne," Clarissa protested.

"Call it an exchange." Marianne hefted the purse in her hands.

"What we gave you wouldn't buy a single one of these gowns!" Diana exclaimed, trying to hand them back, but Marianne refused to accept.

"You are incorrect, my dear girls. You have given me my freedom. I cannot take these with me, and I would far rather have you wear them than let them moulder away here. Everything I leave behind is yours; I give it to you freely."

Overcome, both girls pressed close to embrace her and thank her profusely, but Marianne knew they had given her the greater gift.

Chapter Five

Havers Hall, Herefordshire
Mid December, 1819

Five days later, Marianne walked slowly up the long tree-lined carriageway to Havers Hall, her bag weighing heavily on her weary arm. It had been a long, cold, exhausting trip from Creighton, and the last leg had been the worst; she had paid a farmer returning from Worcester to Haverford to give her a ride, but he had dropped her at the end of the carriageway with a remark in an accent so thick she hadn't understood more than one word in two.

Two of the words had been 'Havers Hall,' though, and combined with his pointing finger and cheerful smile, she had taken it to mean the end of her journey was finally approaching.

A half-mile walk was the last thing she wanted, but she had little choice. Summoning the last of her internal fortitude, and praying Ellen and Thomas were at home, she trudged up the long gravelled way, almost too weary to appreciate the beautiful house coming into view.

Havers Hall was a large building of golden stone, which would have likely glowed in the sunshine on a summer's day, but still managed to look magnificent even on a grey December day with rain clouds threatening. The closer she got, the more intimidating the house looked, and Marianne found herself nervous of her reception as she climbed the wide, shallow steps to the huge double doors at the main entryway.

Maybe they'll tell me to go around the back, to the servants' entrance, she thought with a small giggle to herself. She was wearing one of her plainest gowns, a dark grey wool practical for travelling but hardly glamorous.

The door opened promptly to her knock, and an imperious-looking butler inspected her from head to toe before saying, "May I assist you, madam?"

"Marianne, Lady Creighton." She tried for her best imperious tone in return and must have achieved it in some measure at least, because the butler looked slightly surprised and immediately stepped aside to welcome her into the house.

"I do beg your pardon, my lady. I understood you were not expected for another week or so, but Lord and Lady Havers will undoubtedly be delighted to welcome you."

"Thank you," Marianne murmured, relieved.

"I am Allsopp, the butler. May I take your bag? The, ah, rest of your luggage?"

"Later, Allsopp," she murmured, allowing him to slip the bag from her frozen fingers with a sense of relief.

He stepped aside with it and tugged on a bell cord, and moments later a footman entered the grand hallway. "Matthew, please advise her ladyship that her guest, Lady Creighton, has arrived ahead of schedule."

The order became redundant a moment later, as Ellen, Lady Havers, descended the stairs, dressed in a blue gown one would think far too simple for a lady of her rank if one was not acquainted with Ellen herself. A smile came to Marianne's weary face at the sight of her friend; it seemed Ellen had not changed in essentials even though she was now a countess.

"Marianne?" Ellen said disbelievingly.

I must look a fright, Marianne thought, *pale, weary and dirty with road-dust*. Ellen's delight at seeing her was genuine, however, and she found herself drawn into a close embrace.

"Dear Marianne, you didn't send word you'd be arriving early! In fact, we haven't received any letter from you at all; I hoped you would accept the invitation… why, you're shaking with cold! Come into the library, it's lovely and warm in there. Have some hot tea sent in immediately, Allsopp, and whatever Cook can rustle up quickly to warm Lady Creighton, please."

"At once, my lady," Allsopp said to their backs as Ellen put her arm around Marianne and led her through a door into a beautiful library, light and airy, quite unlike the dark-panelled, musty room at Creighton Hall. A fire crackled merrily in the grate. Marianne soon found herself pressed to sit down in a comfortable chair, Ellen scooping up a shawl from the back of another chair close by and settling it around her shoulders.

"There, we'll soon have you warm. I'm so glad to see you."

Marianne felt quite ridiculous for being brought to tears by Ellen's joyous welcome, but she could not prevent the fat drops which threatened to spill.

Perceptive and kind, Ellen saw her distress and immediately pressed a handkerchief into her hands. "Hush, now. You're tired and overset. We'll have some hot tea and you can tell me everything later."

Grateful when Ellen didn't press her, Marianne slowly regained her composure over tea and scones, warm from the oven and dripping with butter and jam. She took the time to survey her friend, thinking that marriage very clearly suited Ellen. The young countess fairly glowed, and though the cut of her gown was simple, Marianne noticed now the quality of the fabric and the delicate embroidery one shade darker than the fine wool which decorated the bodice. Her brown hair was beautifully curled and arranged, braids looping around her head in a coronet, while her changeable, sea-coloured eyes were bright with happiness.

Envy twisted in Marianne's gut, and she looked down at her teacup, silently chiding herself. Ellen deserved her happiness. She'd lost her parents, her home, everything. If Thomas hadn't inherited the earldom almost by sheer luck and fallen in love with his distant cousin, who knew what circumstances Ellen might have been reduced to? At least Marianne had never had to worry about having a roof over her head, even now.

53

"My housekeeper will have your suite aired and warm by now," Ellen said as they finished their tea, "so let me take you up and you can refresh yourself. Will you come down to dinner tonight, or take a tray in your room? It is only Thomas and me at present, since our other guests aren't expected to arrive until next week, but we should be delighted to have your company. And then, perhaps, you might wish to tell us what has you arriving on our doorstep in such a state, alone, with only one small bag?"

Ellen's words were gentle, but they caused another surge of guilt in Marianne. "Yes," she agreed, looking up to meet her friend's kind smile. "Yes, I'd love to join you both for dinner, and I'll tell you everything then."

Marianne had brought one nice gown with her, a lavender silk which rolled up surprisingly small. The lady's maid Ellen had sent to attend her pressed it while Marianne luxuriated in a copper tub filled with steaming water and aromatic soap, soaking off the grime of travel and allowing her strained nerves to unwind. She had barely slept since leaving Creighton, and the feeling of finally being safe and warm had her eyelids drooping with weariness.

"My lady," the maid said quietly, "shall I rinse your hair, now? Else there will be too little time to dry it before dinner."

"Yes, thank you," Marianne said, pushing herself to sit forward a little reluctantly. "I'm sorry, I didn't catch your name, earlier?"

"Jean, my lady." She had good hands, gentle as she washed out Marianne's long, wavy auburn hair and combed out the tangles, squeezing it firmly in a thick piece of linen to squeeze out as much water as possible before helping Marianne from the tub and swathing her in a beautiful silk dressing-gown which had certainly not been in Marianne's small bag.

"Come sit by the fire, my lady, and let's dry that hair off," Jean encouraged, and Marianne followed, only too pleased to sink into the comfortably upholstered chair and curl her feet up beneath her, tilting her head towards the flames.

She must have drowsed off while Jean went back to pressing her gown and dealing with her other clothes, all of which needed laundering, because the next thing she knew, Jean was gently waking her and her hair was quite dry.

"You do seem very tired, my lady. Are you sure you wouldn't like a tray here and to go straight to bed? I'm sure the Earl and the Countess wouldn't mind…"

"No, no," Marianne waved off Jean's concern. "I thank you, but I feel much refreshed after that little rest, and I am looking forward to seeing Lord Havers again." Her stomach chose that moment to let out a loud rumble, and she chuckled. "I admit to feeling rather famished, too!"

"As you wish, my lady," Jean said with a small laugh. "How would you like me to do your hair?"

Not wanting to put Jean to too much trouble, Marianne settled for a simple coil of braids at the nape of her neck, a few curls hanging loose at the side of her face. Not for the first time, she was grateful for her naturally wavy hair; it took a curl very easily and needed little work to be arranged into any fashionable style she pleased.

Very soon, she was following the same young footman who had taken her bag on her arrival along the twisting hallways of the grand old manor house, admiring the paintings on the walls, the beautifully polished wooden floors and thick carpets, the immaculate cleanliness of everything. "It must take an army of servants to keep the Hall in this condition," Marianne mused aloud.

"Lord and Lady Havers turn away no one who needs employment," the footman answered her, a little to her surprise. "They have begun a programme of training young men and women who wish to enter service, and servants trained at Havers Hall are now in high demand throughout the county. A school in the village has been opened, too, and all the local boys and girls are learning to read and write."

The footman sounded quite incredulous, and Marianne supposed it was quite unheard-of to teach common-born children their letters. Especially the girls. It sounded very much like the thoughtful Ellen she knew and her egalitarian American husband, though. "How wonderful," she said encouragingly as they descended the grand staircase. "And are you one of these trainees?"

"Yes, my lady. Is it so obvious?" He looked quite dismayed, and she tried not to laugh.

"Not at all, I should never have guessed. I was merely curious," she said kindly, though in truth most footmen would not have spoken to her unless she asked them a direct question. Undoubtedly, the young man would learn that rule as he completed his training, though she found his relaxed, informative attitude quite refreshing.

Allsopp, the butler, was in the hall at the foot of the stairs, and he bowed low to her as she descended the last step. "Good evening, Lady Creighton. Lord and Lady Havers await you in the parlour." He gestured for her to follow him.

Thomas and Ellen stood by the fire, deep in conversation, but they at once broke off with welcoming smiles as Allsopp conducted Marianne into the parlour and formally announced her.

"Lady Creighton, it is delightful to see you again." Thomas bowed formally over her hand. "Ellen is overjoyed you were able to come so soon."

Marianne smiled at him. "I am overjoyed to be here… and please, call me Marianne. Since I am imposing on your hospitality without notice, it seems rather ridiculous to insist on the formalities."

Thomas chuckled and nodded. "I'm sure you know formal address doesn't come easily to me anyway," he said frankly, "so I'm very happy to hear you say that, Marianne. You must call me Thomas, of course."

"Of course," she echoed, and let Ellen take her hand and draw her closer to the fire while Thomas poured her a glass of sherry to savour before dinner.

With the warmth of their welcome and an excellent dinner set before her, Marianne felt comfortable and safe enough to slowly reveal what had led her to depart Creighton with such haste and secrecy. Ellen was vocally outraged on her behalf, proclaiming herself disgusted with Arthur and Lavinia for attempting to ban Marianne from London.

"Your nieces sound like dear girls, though!" Ellen declared as Marianne explained how Diana and Clarissa had made her escape possible. "I look forward to meeting them in London, and of course you must accompany us there, and remain with us for the Season. You are welcome to stay with us for as long as you wish, dearest, for life if need be. And please believe me when I say that I certainly do not expect you to act as an unpaid governess or companion! In fact, if you would be interested," she cast a glance at Thomas, who nodded benignly, "there are a number of young women in Haverford who would definitely benefit from exposure to a lady of your quality and talents. I have no doubt we could find some paying work for you, if you wished it."

"I would very much appreciate that," Marianne said stoutly, though she had never worked a day in her life.

Thomas gave her a perceptive look, but said nothing as Ellen went on.

"In fact, if you would be willing, I would greatly appreciate your advice myself. I have never hosted a house party, and there are a thousand and one ways I could make a spectacular social misstep. Your assistance would be invaluable... Thomas, dear, could you find out the going rate for a paid companion? I want to make sure I am not taking advantage of Marianne..."

"Certainly not," Marianne said at the same time as Thomas said;

"Of course, my love."

"I could not accept payment for helping you, Ellen," Marianne continued. "Please consider it my thanks for your most generous hospitality. Anything I can do to assist you, please, you need only ask."

"I most certainly will." Ellen's smile was a little cheeky. "You may regret such a generous offer!"

"Never." Grateful beyond measure for Ellen's kindness and understanding, Marianne reached out to clasp her hand. "Thank you," she said softly, glancing from Ellen to Thomas and back again. "Thank you both so much."

"You're very welcome," Thomas spoke for both of them, and Ellen squeezed Marianne's hand in return. "What are friends for, after all?"

Chapter Six

I am lucky beyond belief to have such friends, Marianne mused as she let Jean dress her hair the following morning. Though she had only a plain gown to wear, it had been freshly washed, pressed, and returned to her that morning looking like new. She thanked Jean profusely, but the maid merely looked surprised before advising her Havers Hall had a positive surfeit of laundry maids who were more than happy to assist her.

"Will the rest of your wardrobe be arriving soon, my lady?" Jean enquired delicately as she inserted the last hairpin to support the arrangement of braids she had deftly woven from Marianne's thick auburn hair.

"I'm afraid not," Marianne admitted.

Jean pursed her lips thoughtfully. "You're taller than Lady Havers, but more of a size with Lady Louisa, the last Earl's daughter," she said. "Caused a dreadful scandal last year, she did, running off with a footman from the London house. Left quite a wardrobe behind. Perhaps you might speak to Lady Havers about adjusting some of the things for your use?"

"I couldn't possibly," Marianne disclaimed, but she thought wistfully of the stunning gowns Lady Louisa Havers had been wont to wear. Thomas' cousin, Louisa had hoped to become the next Countess of Havers by marriage to Thomas, but he had chosen Ellen instead and Louisa had disappeared in a scandal which had been the talk of London... at least until Marianne's husband dropped dead the day after Thomas and Ellen's wedding.

Jean looked thoughtful rather than accepting of Marianne's refusal, and Marianne suspected the maid intended to approach the topic through a roundabout method, quite possibly via Ellen's personal maid. Well, so be it. Marianne certainly could not ask herself, even though she would like something more elegant to wear.

Another young footman waited outside her door to escort her to the breakfast room, a completely different room from the one where they had eaten dinner last night, which Marianne learned now was called the Oak Dining Room, on account of the oak-panelled walls. There was also the Grand Dining Room, for when more than twenty were expected to dine.

"And are more than twenty expected at the house party?" Marianne enquired of the chatty young man. She had not attended such a large gathering since leaving London last year in the wake of her husband's death.

"Not to stay at the Hall, no, my lady, but there are several occasions planned where more will be invited. Local gentry, you understand."

"Indeed," Marianne agreed, finding herself looking forward to the house party with enthusiasm. She had always enjoyed social events, though her pleasure had usually been curtailed by her husband's severe restrictions. To have the freedom to dance and talk with whomever she pleased, male or female, was a much-longed-for treat.

Ellen was alone in the breakfast room, eating muffins spread with blackberry jam, when Marianne entered.

"Good morning!" Ellen exclaimed, pushing aside the newspaper she had been perusing. "Do sit down." She waved at the seat beside her. "Would you like tea, coffee, or chocolate? Hugh will bring you some fresh. And please let Jacob know what you would like for breakfast."

Two different footmen stood ready to leap to her command, Marianne noted with amusement. Ellen must spend her days thinking up tasks to keep all her staff busy. No wonder everything in the Hall looked so perfect.

"Tea would be delightful, thank you," she told Hugh then turned to the other footman, "and I have a weakness for coddled eggs with buttered toast, if that wouldn't be too much trouble for your cook?"

"Not at all, my lady." Jacob bowed, and Ellen and Marianne were left briefly alone as the two footmen left hastily to fetch her breakfast.

Ellen smiled warmly at her as Marianne settled into her chair, and then to Marianne's utmost surprise she said, "What would you like to do today?"

Marianne stared at her, mouth dropping open. She stared so long Ellen began to fidget, obviously becoming a little uncomfortable.

"Is something wrong, Marianne?"

"I was trying to remember the last time I was asked that question," Marianne said with some difficulty, feeling tears welling, "and do you know, I don't think anyone has *ever* asked me that."

"Oh!" Ellen's hand flew to her mouth. In her eyes, brimming with sympathy, Marianne saw her friend comprehended the depth of what her question meant. A choice, given freely to someone who had never had any.

The return of Hugh with Marianne's tea put paid to the moment of emotion, though Marianne still had to take several sips and some deep breaths before she felt able to speak again. "What do you suggest?" she asked Ellen. "I should love a tour of the Hall, but if you have any other ideas, I am all agog to hear them."

"A tour sounds just the thing," Ellen said encouragingly, "particularly since it is set to rain all day today. After a year living here, I think I have my way around all figured out, at least. Or at last, I should say. I cannot tell you how many times I have got lost; Allsopp has had to send out more than one search party for me!"

Marianne laughed, as Ellen had obviously intended her to. "These huge old houses are the devil, aren't they? Creighton Hall is much the same. While the front elevation looks both coherent and elegant, behind there is often a hodgepodge of alterations and additions which make the house into an absolute muddle."

"Indeed," Ellen nodded, "and despite having all the money in the world, the old Earl was an utter miser. He closed off half the Hall, didn't employ enough servants to keep the rooms in good condition, and let them fall into disrepair. Thomas and I have been opening them up, redecorating, and commissioning new furniture, carpets, and curtains from local makers. With everything finally complete, we thought a house party a nice way to celebrate having the Hall fully open again."

"Very nice," Marianne agreed.

"But I do need your advice. Thomas hasn't a clue, of course, and I… well, precedence is a bit of a mystery to me, still. It's always been everyone else above, then me definitely at the bottom." Ellen smiled wistfully. "I have no idea who should get the best guest suite: a dowager duchess or a marquis? Does the widowed sister of an impoverished earl come above the wealthy heir to a viscountcy?"

"The duchess, and yes, she would, because ladies always come before gentlemen," Marianne said, laughing when Ellen looked dismayed.

"Thank God you did come early! I have it all wrong!"

"We'll soon have it all sorted out," Marianne promised as her breakfast was set before her with great ceremony. "As soon as I've done justice to this marvellous breakfast, you can go fetch whatever notes you have, and we'll get to work."

With Marianne's experienced assistance and an army of servants only too willing to jump to her slightest request, Ellen soon had a plan for accommodating her incoming guests she was much more confident about. They spent the entire morning touring the house, examining the bedrooms and the linen, before discovering themselves quite famished when Allsopp appeared to delicately suggest they might wish to take a break for a light nuncheon which Cook had prepared for them.

"Is it near noon already?" Ellen asked, startled.

"I think it must be, for my stomach has been rumbling this last half-hour at least," Marianne admitted.

Tucking her arm through Marianne's, Ellen smiled. "I am an abominable hostess, as you see. Here less than a day, and already I am overworking and starving you!"

"Nonsense." Marianne laughed at Ellen's teasing. "I am delighted to be of use, I promise, and I find myself looking forward to meeting your guests."

"Well, we will be an eclectic gathering." Ellen led her back through the confusing maze of corridors to the central part of the house, and to the pretty parlour where they had taken breakfast. "I hope to make it something of a tradition, to gather at Havers Hall for a Christmas house party."

"A charming idea, and you may count on my future attendance. If I am invited, that is," Marianne added.

"Of course you are, and in future I will be instructing Thomas to send the coach for you, too, so that any further issues with transportation will be avoided!" Ellen was quite indignant on Marianne's behalf, outraged that Arthur and Lavinia had denied her request to travel and effectively tried to turn her into an unpaid companion to their children.

"Thank you, my dear," Marianne said, squeezing Ellen's arm gratefully before letting go and taking her seat at the table.

Thomas came in to join them, and Ellen jumped to her feet to greet him, her face aglow. They shared a discreet kiss before taking their seats.

"How have you spent the morning, ladies?" Thomas asked as the footmen served them soup and bread, pouring cups of a cloudy apple cider which, served warm, was absolutely delicious. Marianne was unaccustomed to eating a proper meal at this time of day, but it was a pleasant idea, she found, and she was hungry from their exertions that morning.

Marianne sipped at her cup while Ellen expounded on their activities and Thomas listened with every appearance of interest, adding a few remarks now and then. He had apparently spent the morning with one of the tenant farmers, discussing that year's crop yields and what seeds would be planted at the next harvest.

Marianne could not remember her husband ever concerning himself with anything so mundane, so workmanlike. He had left all such decisions to his land steward, content merely to count the profits and apportion some of them to his investment advisers. Another portion had been assigned to Marianne, with new gowns produced for her by London's finest modistes every week. She had been nothing more to him than an ornament, something beautiful and expensive which nobody else could have. He had never encouraged her to take any part in the running of the household, though she was a viscount's daughter and had been well-trained in the management of a great house.

Helping Ellen today was the most fulfilling thing Marianne had been permitted to do in years, and she found herself hoping Ellen would keep wanting her input and advice throughout the house party.

This must be what it's like to have a brother and sister, Marianne thought as the meal went on and Thomas and Ellen included her happily in their chatter. Her brother had died fighting Napoleon when she was only thirteen, and he had been five years older, so she remembered him but little. Perhaps if he had lived, they could have been friends, at least.

She felt so very comfortable with Thomas and Ellen, confident she could tell them anything or ask for their help and have it freely given, without expectation of repayment. When Thomas offhandedly advised her he had sent two servants and a coach to collect her wardrobe from Cumbria and they should return before the house party began in earnest; Marianne was hard put to keep the tears from flowing.

It turned out you didn't need to ask, sometimes.

Chapter Seven

A week later, Marianne felt as though she had been living at Havers Hall for half her life. On first name terms with every member of the (very extensive) staff, she now knew her way around the beautiful old house as well as Thomas and Ellen did. If she didn't quite recall the name of every Havers ancestor in the portrait gallery, well, they weren't *her* ancestors.

Marianne sat with Ellen in the large, beautifully-appointed front parlour where guests were usually received. The first guests for the house party were expected today, but at the moment since Thomas was out and about the estate it was just the two of them waiting, both settled in comfortable chairs by the fire with books in hand.

Reading was another joy Marianne had rediscovered. Creighton had all but forbidden it to her, not permitting her to purchase any books or join a lending library and refusing her access to his own library. Ellen, however, was a dedicated bookworm, as was Thomas, and they both liked to spend at least an hour or two a day comfortably ensconced with a book. Ellen had encouraged her to select anything she fancied from their eclectic collection, and Marianne had soon found herself enjoying that quiet hour spent between the pages, discovering the wondrous worlds which lived within the imagination.

The sound of hooves and carriage wheels caused both women to look up, and Marianne slipped a ribbon between the pages and closed her book regretfully.

"You can finish it later," Ellen said with a smile, obviously seeing her regret.

"I'm enjoying it very much, I must admit. Turning down two suitors! Elizabeth Bennet was lucky indeed to have a supportive father who did not make her marry Mr. Collins, but I do hope her mother does not find out she turned Mr. Darcy down as well."

Ellen laughed. "I will not spoil the plot for you, but I'm very glad you are enjoying it. I thought you would appreciate a story where the heroine gets the opportunity to say no - and to tell her unsuitable suitors precisely what she thinks of them!"

"Indeed, I do." Marianne sighed happily. "I shall be honest - the greatest pleasure I am deriving from it is the certain knowledge that Creighton would have flown into a rage at the mere suggestion I should be permitted to read it."

Ellen snickered. Over the last few days, they had become close enough that Marianne felt safe confiding in Ellen how much she had hated her husband, despised and feared him. There were some things about her marriage she doubted she would ever be able to talk about, but in a way, telling Ellen what she could had been cathartic. As they walked down the stairs to the front hall Marianne thought again how glad she was that Ellen had sat down beside her in the wallflowers' corner where Marianne had been hiding from her husband at the ball where they'd first met.

Allsopp was opening the doors, with two footmen at the ready to hurry down the steps and assist the guests from the carriage drawing to a stop. Four handsome bay horses drew a carriage of superior quality, obviously very new, but with no family crest upon the doors. *New money*, Marianne assessed. Not that she cared. Creighton's money was very old, and she despised every adult male member of that bloodline.

"The Alleynes," Ellen murmured as a footman opened the carriage door and a handsome woman in late middle age, wearing a serviceable gown under a heavy woollen cloak, stepped down with a welcoming smile.

"I don't think I know them." Marianne watched as a gentleman with a balding pate and a kindly face stepped down next.

"Sir Tobias and Lady Alleyne - Isabelle. Their daughter Leonora made her debut this autumn. She's a confirmed wallflower, but has the most beautiful singing voice; I will be begging her to entertain us in the evenings."

Leonora was obviously the young lady stepping down with a shy smile and a word of thanks for the footman assisting her. With mouse-brown hair, a round pink face, and a figure a little too plump for fashion, Marianne could see why the girl was a wallflower. She would be no competition for the beauties of the Ton.

"She looks sweet. I shall be glad to know her and her parents."

Ellen shot her a grateful look as the family ascended the steps to join them. They had been joined by a young man of about twenty years of age.

Tall and thin, he had the same mouse-brown hair as Leonora.

"Welcome to Havers Hall," Ellen said.

"Lady Havers," Lady Alleyne said. "It is so good to see you again. Havers Hall is even more beautiful than I imagined. Please allow me to present our son, Joseph."

"A pleasure to meet you, Mr. Alleyne." Ellen offered her hand and Joseph bowed quite correctly over it. Marianne was very proud of Ellen then as her friend remembered the proper way to introduce persons of a lower rank to her; she turned to Marianne and said, "Lady Creighton, please allow me to introduce my friends Sir Tobias and Lady Alleyne, and their children Mr. and Miss Alleyne. Marianne, Lady Creighton," she turned back to the Alleynes, who bowed and curtseyed.

"It is a pleasure to meet any friend of Ellen's," Marianne said with a warm smile, offering her hand to Lady Alleyne, who looked a little overawed as she touched Marianne's fingers lightly. "I am delighted to make your acquaintances."

"Oh, we are most honoured to make your acquaintance, Lady Creighton!" Lady Alleyne gushed, her eyes taking in every detail of Marianne's appearance. "Leonora, do make your bows, girl. And Joseph!" She looked to her son, who was staring at Marianne as though he had suddenly glimpsed Paradise. "Oh… I believe I have forgot something in the carriage. Joseph!" Succeeding in obtaining his attention, she sent him back for a handkerchief, even though Marianne could clearly see one peeking from her sleeve, and carried on talking without missing a beat, commenting on everything from the state of the roads to the charms of the rustic inn where they had stayed the night before.

Introductions made and Lady Alleyne finally running out of steam on her commentary, Ellen ushered the Alleynes inside and directed waiting maids to escort her newly arrived guests to the suites she had allotted them.

"We should be delighted if you would join us for a light nuncheon at one o'clock?" Ellen invited, and Lady Alleyne accepted for the family, declaring they would wash up and be down directly.

"They seem nice," Marianne remarked as she and Ellen returned to the parlour.

"They are; I requested an introduction to Leonora after I heard her sing and was delighted with her. She looks a mousy little thing, but is very witty and clever. Sir Tobias invented a new type of ammunition during the war, for which he received his knighthood, and has invented any number of other clever things. I am always utterly fascinated by his conversation, when you can get him to talk."

Which might be a little bit trying when Lady Alleyne is present, Marianne surmised. The woman seemed rather on the chatty side, though nice enough.

They were just reaching for their books when the sound of another carriage's wheels had Ellen rising to her feet again.

"You need not come down, if you wish," she said. "I would not drag you up and down stairs all day, every time another guest arrives!"

"I will accompany you until Thomas gets back from his visit with the tenant," Marianne compromised. "After that, he can climb all those stairs with you!"

Ellen laughed. "I am always glad of your company," she said warmly, and they set off again.

The change in sound disturbed Alex, and he looked up from his book. The carriage wheels were crunching on gravel now, rather than the packed dirt of the road. The horses slowed, which told him they were likely arriving at Havers Hall.

Setting the book down on the seat, he peered out of the window, admiring the handsome larch trees lining the broad avenue leading up to a beautiful house built of golden Cotswold stone. Even on a dull, grey December day, the house had a warm and welcoming look.

"A pretty prospect," Alex murmured to himself, startling his valet awake from his snooze.

"Beg your pardon, m'lord?"

"I believe we are arrived, Simons."

"So soon? Why, we left Worcester just a little while ago!"

Alex hid a smile. Simons was in his late sixties and definitely nearing retirement. He was also fanatically loyal to Alex and extremely protective of his master's privacy, which was why Alex would never dream of going anywhere without him.

"It is nearing noon, Simons," Alex said when he had recovered his countenance. "We have made good time, though. The roads in this part of the country are certainly better maintained than those in the far north."

"Indeed." Simons peered out of the other window. "Very handsome grounds," he approved. "I count no less than four gardeners attending to that shrubbery yonder - in the depth of winter, too! Let us hope the house is equally well-cared for."

"And the stables." Alex turned his head to check on his horse, following behind the carriage, its lead line held by one of his grooms aside another horse. "Else Julius will likely wreak havoc."

"Don't know why you keep that animal," Simons grumbled. "Troublesome beast."

"He saved my life too many times to count on the Continent. I'll not abandon him now."

Simons humphed as the carriage finally drew to a halt. Two footmen immediately approached the door and opened it, placing a step for them to disembark. "Attentive, at least," Simons mumbled from his corner. "Go ahead, m'lord. I'll see to your things."

"Don't be lifting anything yourself," Alex said, receiving a narrow-eyed glare in return. Turning away to cover another smile, he stepped down from the carriage with a nod of thanks to the footmen and started up the steps to the Hall. Three steps up, he raised his gaze to the two women standing at the door and promptly stubbed his toe on the next step.

His only consolation, as he bit back a yelp of pain, was that Marianne looked far more shocked to see him than he was surprised to see her standing arm-in-arm with Ellen Havers. He had, after all, known she was going to be there, and from her expression she had not put together the Marquis of Glenkellie with Alexander Rotherhithe. When he had known her, he was only a very distant relation, never expected to ascend to the title.

"My lord." The Countess of Havers curtseyed gracefully as he arrived at the top of the steps, and Marianne perforce followed suit, though she had blanched pale.

"Lady Havers." Alex bowed deep in return. "Lady Creighton."

"Oh, you are acquainted with Marianne? How silly of me; of course you are! With you not in London this year, I forgot you lived there for several years and know everyone." Ellen turned to Marianne with a friendly smile, placing her hand on Marianne's arm.

"It has been many years since Lady Creighton and I last met," Alex said after a full minute of awkward silence. "Indeed, she was then merely Miss Abingdon, daughter of a viscount, and I... nobody of consequence at all."

He had not thought it possible Marianne could turn any paler, but her skin took on the hue of ash, and she swayed a little. Kind, thoughtful Ellen noticed at once, of course, and urged her friend inside, back into the warmth.

Alex found himself delegated to the care of a very proper butler, who promptly escorted him to a handsome guest suite on the second floor with sweeping views across a valley to the west of the house, a winding river at the bottom, and thick woods on the hill beyond.

It was quite lovely, and he was still standing at the window admiring the vista when Simons arrived with four sturdy footmen carrying Alex's trunks. Simons looked quite in his element as he directed the men, and a moment later extended his sway to two more who arrived bearing jugs of hot water for Alex to wash.

"A nuncheon will be served at noon, my lord," one of the footmen advised, "and Lord Havers is expected back in time for it."

"Indeed," Alex murmured, "I believe I see him now." A horse had entered the picturesque view outside, cantering along the river to a crossing point. The rider was still a little too far away to make out his identity, but his coat and hat were clearly those of a gentleman. Perhaps a half-mile distant, the horse and rider would reach the house in no time at all, and therefore Alex should also waste little time in changing his clothes and washing off the dust of travel.

He wondered if Marianne would attend the nuncheon, or if she would cry off after obviously having been surprised by his arrival. Perhaps she would plead illness.

His jaw tightened as he turned away from the prospect beyond the window. She could not avoid him indefinitely, not at a house party expected to last a full fortnight.

Sooner rather than later, they would have the conversation which had been postponed for too many years - and he would have his answer as to why she had lied to his face and broken his youthful heart.

Chapter Eight

Claiming a sudden sick headache, Marianne retreated immediately to her rooms, grateful for Ellen's kindly disposition. She was quite certain Ellen suspected her illness coming upon her at the same time as the Marquis of Glenkellie's arrival was no coincidence, but Marianne was in no way ready to explain her prior connection with Alexander Rotherhithe.

Lying down, she allowed Jean to place a damp cloth over her brow and then pleaded to be left alone. She needed to think.

Jean retreated only as far as her dressing room, leaving the door cracked open so she would hear if Marianne called for her, but that was far enough. In silence and blissful solitude, Marianne tried to come up with a method by which she might somehow avoid being in a room with Alexander Rotherhithe for the next two weeks.

A headache was coming on in earnest as she tried to find a way out of her dilemma. If only she still had access to the Creighton fortune! But even if she wrote a letter to Arthur, she doubted he would send for her. And she could not possibly ask Ellen and Thomas to convey her back to Cumbria.

She had friends who would take her in - at least she hoped she did - but getting to them without funds was another matter. Running away was not an option open to her, even if her pride would permit it. Ellen would be convinced something dreadful had happened to her, besides, and that was no way for Marianne to repay Ellen's kindness.

Somehow, she was going to have to face Alexander and live with his contempt. She'd seen the disgust in his eyes as he looked at her. So far as he knew, she'd broken their secret engagement a mere three weeks after he sailed for Spain to marry another man: a much older, much wealthier, titled man.

It was a cruel twist of fate that Alexander was now both wealthier and better titled than her husband had ever been. If only her father had known! He might have let her 'throw herself away on a mere Mister' after all.

If the last eight years had taught her anything, it was that there was no use crying over spilt milk. Lying still and silent, Marianne reconciled herself to facing Alexander and being civil to him. She was no longer the naive girl he had cared for; she was a grown woman, married and widowed. She would not be intimidated by contemptuous stares, even though Alexander Rotherhithe had grown up into a very impressive man indeed.

Tall and slender as a young man, maturity and his years as a soldier had added muscle and breadth to that long frame. And the scar on his cheek only added to his dark, wickedly handsome looks as far as she was concerned.

Unconsciously, Marianne lifted her hand to her own cheek, wondering how exactly Alex had received the scar. Though it had faded to pink now, it must have been a terrible wound when he'd first received it, flaying his cheek open to the bone and barely missing his eye. It was hardly something she could ask him, especially as she planned to avoid being in his company as much as she could possibly manage!

The sound of carriage wheels outside again brought a smile to her face. With more than twenty guests to stay at the Hall and more coming from the local area each day for activities and dinners, surely there would be enough people around that she need never find herself alone with Alexander. She could hide behind a shield of politeness and sociability, much as she had hidden her feelings behind a polished social facade when Creighton paraded her around London as his trophy bride.

She could do this.

What choice did she have, after all?

The Earl of Havers grinned as Alex entered the drawing room. "Glenkellie. Glad you decided to come."

"So am I," Alex said honestly, shaking Thomas' offered hand. "Havers Hall is beautiful; my compliments on your home. My valet is in heaven with such facilities at his disposal."

"You can thank my predecessor for most of the Hall's amenities," Thomas admitted. "He liked his luxuries."

"It's not your predecessor who employs a veritable army of staff though, is it?" Alex raised his brows. As the owner of a large estate of his own, he knew the Hall was definitely overstaffed.

"I wanted to talk to you about that, actually. I'm thinking of starting a proper training academy, staffed by experienced mentors who are getting a little long in the tooth for heavy work but have a wealth of knowledge to pass on."

"For house servants?"

"For all kinds of skilled tradespersons. The current system of one apprentice per tradesman - and that's if they're willing to take one on - doesn't increase the supply of skilled workers, does it?"

"I suppose not," Alex conceded. "Where do I come in?"

"I'm looking for investors, of course." Thomas grinned irrepressibly.

"Naturally. Well, if you have a proposal, I'll take a look at it." Alex had no problem with the idea of going into business with Thomas; there were few people he could say that about, but the American earl had proved himself both financially astute and compassionate towards those of lesser consequence to himself.

"Do not start talking business now, Thomas." Ellen came up beside them, resting a hand on her husband's arm.

He placed his own hand over her fingers and gave her an apologetic smile. "Sorry, my love."

"You must let me introduce Lord Glenkellie to our other guests," she reproved gently. "Or are you already acquainted with the Alleynes, my lord?"

"I am not, but I should be honoured to meet any friends of yours, Lady Havers," Alex said gallantly. "I already know Lady Creighton, of course. Where is she, by the way?"

Ellen's glance was sharp. "Resting," she said a little curtly. "She was feeling unwell. Should she be recovered enough, she may rejoin us at dinner."

"I didn't know you were acquainted with Lady Creighton, Glenkellie," Thomas said, his expression surprised.

"It was a long time ago," Alex demurred. "I daresay I don't know the person she is now at all."

Had he ever known her? He had to wonder, even as one part of his mind remained focused on remaining polite as Ellen introduced him to the Alleyne family. Miss Alleyne looked quite overawed and said not a word, which at least meant she was unlikely to pursue him, though her mother positively fawned over him. He was used to that and tuned it out by thinking of Marianne, of the look on her face as she'd recognised him. He'd changed from the young boy she'd known when they were children playing together before he was sent away to school, even from the stripling lad she'd led on that fatal summer. He was grown up now, hardened by war and life.

Of course, she'd changed too. She'd been a lovely child, but at eighteen, she was the prettiest girl he'd ever seen -- fresh and beautiful as a sunrise. Every head had turned when Marianne Abingdon entered a room; she'd had every man in London panting after her.

Alex, a lowly lieutenant with no honorifics before his name, had never got close enough to speak a word to the perfect Miss Abingdon, despite their prior acquaintance. Not until the night when he'd stepped out of an overcrowded ballroom, head spinning from heat and one too many glasses of champagne, and walked through a garden in the darkness looking for somewhere to take a rest. On a stone bench beneath a weeping willow, Marianne Abingdon had been seated, her hands braced behind her, leaning back to gaze up at the sky.

Alex froze, shocked, a few steps away, wondering whether he should back away. Was she waiting for someone?

"I can't see the stars," she said after a few moments, making him jump.

"It's the smoke from the manufactories," Alex replied finally when she said nothing more, and she turned her head to look at him. Realising he stood in shadow beneath the trees, he moved forward, into the bright path of moonlight which stopped just short of her bench. "My apologies. I didn't mean to intrude on your privacy."

"That's quite all right. I was about to go back in anyway." Swinging her feet to the ground, she rose gracefully, the sway of her willowy body making his mouth grow dry. Miss Abingdon never wore fancy frills or lace or even strong patterns; she favoured simple white gowns which contrasted spectacularly with her chestnut-red hair and did little to conceal her lissome figure.

"Have we met?" she asked him quite directly.

He bowed, finding it difficult to speak in the face of her incredible beauty. "Not in many years, Miss Abingdon; you were a child when last I saw you and I daresay you do not remember me. Alexander Rotherhithe, at your service."

She tilted her head, examining his uniform, one long curl bobbing against her neck as she did so. "*Lieutenant* Rotherhithe?"

"Yes, my lady."

"And are you lately returned from the Continent or yet to be deployed?"

"Yet to be deployed, my lady," he answered, startled by the question. She seemed intelligent and informed, unlike the other debutantes - and older ladies - he'd met in London. "My regiment does not yet have orders."

"And do you look forward to the fighting, Mr. Rotherhithe?" She began to walk back towards the house, and he fell into step beside her without thinking.

"No."

"No?" She shot a sideways glance at him. "No dreams of glory on the battlefield, of winning the war for England?"

"Several of my friends have already perished on battlefields far from England's shores," he answered her frankly. "I'll consider myself fortunate if I live to see my home again."

"*Finally,*" she sighed, stopping and turning to look him fully in the face. "A young man with something more than sawdust between his ears!"

Alex couldn't help himself; he grinned. "My apologies, my lady, but I was just thinking something very similar about you."

Her laugh was softly musical. "You are forgiven, Lieutenant… if you will dance with me when we return to the ballroom. I am heartily tired of hearing endless plaudits and paeans to my beauty. Some sensible conversation would be most welcome."

He could not wish for anything more. Gallantly, he insisted she re-enter the house first and go to the ladies' retiring rooms to be seen before returning to the ballroom, while he went back in by a different door. The half-hour until he was face to face with her again, taking her hand to lead her into the dance, seemed the longest of his life. Somehow, he'd convinced himself she was merely amusing herself with him in the garden and had no interest in him at all.

So, when Marianne smiled up at him and said in a confidential tone, "How this last half-hour has dragged!" he felt an overwhelming relief.

"It always does, I find, when there is something one is desperately looking forward to. Conversely, I am sure the next ten minutes will pass in the merest winking of an eye."

She made a little moue and wrinkled her nose, nodding in agreement. "No doubt there is some department of mathematicians at Cambridge studying exactly that. Or philosophers, perhaps?"

"Possibly both, being Cambridge," Alex said dryly. "Though in my experience, there is more drinking and socialising done than actual studying."

"What a waste. I wish women were permitted to study at university." Marianne looked at him almost defiantly; he had the distinct impression she was testing him, watching to see what his reaction to such an inflammatory suggestion might be.

"I have no doubt that one day they will be able to," he said. "Though for the sake of my own gender, I hope they either have their own universities or segregated classes. There were distractions enough without the presence of the fairer sex for foolish young men to lose their common sense over."

Marianne laughed, and Alex thought he had passed her test. "I agree," she said. "Though the foolishness would not be entirely on the part of the young men, I think. Young ladies are equally susceptible to being distracted by a handsome face on a tall young man. Especially in a red coat."

Her eyes twinkled up at him, and he laughed, utterly enchanted by her. "May I call upon you?" he asked impulsively.

"Oh, please do," she answered enthusiastically, and his heart was lost.

Chapter Nine

Marianne wished, quite desperately, for the armour of a fine gown in which to clad herself to face Alex, but the servants Thomas had sent to Cumbria had not yet returned with her wardrobe. She had to content herself with the lavender silk gown she had worn every evening since her arrival at Havers Hall. At least Jean was doing a wonderful job in keeping it clean and pressed, ready for her to dress in each evening, but she was definitely coming to despise the colour.

Apparently divining that her mistress was self-conscious about only having the one evening gown, Jean had been producing different accessories every night to dress it up from some store of things somewhere in the Hall. Tonight she had a wide sash of golden silk, some gold ribbons

95

for Marianne's hair, and a long string of creamy pearls.

"They're fakes, m'lady," Jean said the moment Marianne opened her mouth to protest she couldn't borrow valuable pearls from Ellen. "See, they don't even have a proper catch."

"Where did you find them?" Marianne inspected the pearls with interest. She'd never seen fake jewels before.

"Lady Havers has been cleaning out the attics," Jean admitted. "There's all sorts of things up there in old trunks: gowns which must be a hundred years old, bits and pieces of rusty armour, children's sewing samplers, and broken old toys. I don't think anything's been thrown away in the Hall since it was built."

"Quite likely," Marianne conceded, seating herself to let Jean put up her hair. "Is Lady Havers throwing it away, though?"

"Oh no; she don't believe in throwing things away much. Finds a use for near everything, she does. I asked if I could take a few bits and pieces to dress up your things a touch and she said I could take whatever I wanted." Jean beamed proudly. "These gold ribbons will look very well in your hair, m'lady, and the sash brightens the dress up a treat."

"They do," Marianne said warmly. "Thank you, Jean. You've been so thoughtful."

"Oh, I'm just doing my job, m'lady," the maid disclaimed, but she beamed brightly, and Marianne determined then and there she would give Jean at least one or two gowns once her wardrobe arrived. She did not have much in the way of money or trinkets, but the maid would be able to sell the gowns or pick them apart as she pleased. It was small enough repayment for the confidence the maid's ministrations gave her, enough to get her all the way to the foot of the grand stairs, where Allsopp bowed correctly to her before opening the door to the Oriental Parlour.

While Marianne had seen the room, they had not used it before. She assumed Ellen and Thomas had made the decision to remove here due to the increase in numbers. More guests had arrived, she saw as she entered, and this time she was familiar with the new arrivals.

"Lady Creighton!" Mrs. Pembroke almost fell over herself scurrying to Marianne's side, smiling widely. "It is so very good to see you again!"

"Amelia!" Marianne was genuinely delighted in her turn. Amelia Temple had made her debut at the same time as Marianne, and, as a notable heiress, had been a target for fortune hunters. Since Marianne had been targeted by rakes, the pair of them had discovered themselves hiding out in more than one retiring room together.

Amelia had been lucky enough to marry for love, however. While her parents had wanted her to catch a title, she had instead married a mere Mister: a country squire with a small but charming estate in Hampshire and a passion for horses. A passion Amelia shared.

Mr. Pembroke stood behind Amelia now, smiling broadly. Marianne felt unexpected tears prick at the back of her eyes. Creighton had not approved of her friendship with the Pembrokes and had forbidden her any contact beyond the briefest of polite interactions at social events they were all attending. Being able to express her delight at seeing Amelia again without fear of reprimand was a true pleasure.

"It is wonderful to see you." Impulsively, Marianne embraced her friend. "It has been an age since last I saw you. How do you know the Havers?"

"The earl purchased some horses from us. The sweetest mare for Lady Havers, and a top-grade stallion to improve the bloodlines of his tenants' plough horses. When he told Mr.

Pembroke he did not plan to charge his tenants stud fees for the stallion's services, we knew he was someone we should very much like to know better." Amelia beamed. "And Lady Havers is just *delightful*."

"She most certainly is," Thomas agreed, joining them and making Amelia laugh. "I am glad you are already acquainted; it saves me the probable embarrassment of making a mess of the introductions."

Pembroke and Marianne joined in the laughter, and an atmosphere of general gaiety ensued as they began a lovely conversation. The Alleynes entered the room a few minutes later and were persuaded to join them, and then Ellen herself came in accompanied by a young man and woman Marianne did not know. She introduced them as Viscount Thorpington and his sister, Lady Serena Thorpe.

The viscount was a plain-faced man of around thirty, with a stutter he concealed by speaking as little as possible. Lady Serena was around two and twenty by Marianne's estimation and handsome rather than conventionally pretty, tall and sturdy with a thick mane of black hair barely constrained by her pins. With an unfashionable tan, she looked to be the outdoorsy sort who would have no patience with the languid pace of high society life.

Marianne liked Lady Serena immediately, but she could see why she hadn't been a success in London. The Ton matrons wouldn't have approved of her at all, and her brother's speech issues would have made it difficult for him to make many friends too.

"The Marquis of Glenkellie," Allsopp announced from the door, and a hush fell over the room. Miss Leonora Alleyne squealed a little, hand over her mouth and her eyes wide.

Until her brother nudged her with a frown. "Hush, you goose."

"But a *marquis*!" Leonora whispered back.

Marianne gave her an indulgent smile. "I'll tell you a secret about marquises and dukes," she whispered to the younger girl. "They have to use the chamber pot just like the rest of us!"

Leonora promptly developed the giggles, and Lady Serena Thorpe, who was also close enough to overhear, gave a rather horselike snort before muffling her face in a handkerchief. Blue eyes sparkled as she glanced sideways at Marianne, and Marianne gave her a conspiratorial grin, inwardly thankful for the distraction which meant she didn't have to look at Alexander.

Of course, her reprieve was short-lived, as Ellen escorted Alexander around the room to make introductions. Leonora had edged closer to Marianne, obviously reassured by her apparent nonchalance, and she could hardly flee and leave the debutante alone.

"You are, of course, acquainted with Lady Creighton," Ellen said. Alexander nodded, his eyes cold as they met Marianne's. Instinctively, she looked down at the floor, even as she silently chastised herself for cowardice.

Marianne couldn't even meet his eyes, intently examining the pattern woven into the Turkish rug beneath their feet. Gritting his teeth and ordering himself to be patient, Alex forced a smile as Lady Havers presented a blushing debutante.

"Miss Alleyne." Bowing correctly over the girl's hand, Alex resigned himself to social niceties for the time being. He was acquainted with only one other of the guests -- Viscount Thorpington -- and for Thomas and Ellen's sake he must at least try to be agreeable. He would not for the world spoil their first house party, no matter how much he wanted to shake the truth out of Marianne.

He watched her from the corner of his eye all evening. As the highest-ranking lady present, she went into dinner on Thomas' arm and was seated at his right hand, at the other end of the table from where Alex, as the highest-ranking *gentleman* present, was seated at Ellen's right.

Young Mr. Alleyne was seated on Marianne's other side and watched her in wide-eyed awe, the kind which could well turn into infatuated puppy love, Alex thought grimly, determined to nip that in the bud if Marianne should take it into her head to break another young man's heart for her amusement. At least Thomas Havers was infatuated with his own wife and not likely to be susceptible to Marianne's charms, laugh and smile though she might.

Reluctantly, Alex had to admit Marianne was even lovelier now than she had been at eighteen; maturity had only refined her beauty. If he didn't already know how heartless she could be, he'd likely be crawling after her himself. As it was, he found it difficult to look away. Dressed in a muted lavender gown trimmed with gold ribbon, her auburn hair shone like fire, the perfection of her features outlined by the candlelight. Again and again her softly musical laugh came to his ear, and he only realised he was staring at her in utter absorption when Ellen Havers touched his hand lightly, making him start.

"My apologies, Lord Glenkellie. I was wondering if the soup is not to your liking?" Her brow was creased.

Looking down, Alexander saw he'd taken up his soup spoon in his hand and then failed to even taste from the dish in front of him. "I beg your pardon, my lady," he said contritely. "I was distracted."

"So I see," Ellen murmured, and her eyes flickered as she glanced to the other end of the table. "I do hope you will try it, but if there is anything you particularly wish to have prepared, I pray you will let us know."

Ashamed of his poor manners, Alexander tasted the soup and pronounced it excellent and resolved to pay closer attention to both his dinner and his dinner companions. Ellen had been carrying the entire conversation, with quiet Thorpington on her other side, and he should speak as well with Mrs. Pembroke on his other side. Turning to that lady now, he offered a smile, only to be met with an uncomfortably appraising stare.

"I daresay you do not remember me, my lord," Mrs. Pembroke said almost immediately, "but we have met before, though it was many years

103

ago. Just before you went to the Continent with the army, I believe."

"Indeed?" Alex said, guarded. Mrs. Pembroke looked to be almost exactly Marianne's age, but had none of her mesmerising beauty. Instead, she was positively ordinary, with mid-brown hair, brown eyes, a slightly snub nose, and a round face. A quirky smile lent her expression character, however.

"Why, yes, though I was Miss Temple then, and you merely Lieutenant Rotherhithe. I think we were introduced at Lady Smithfield's garden party."

He still didn't recall the introduction, though he did remember with awful clarity sneaking off from that garden party for a clandestine meeting in a glade of trees with Marianne. A meeting where he'd kissed her for the first time and sworn his undying devotion.

"Ah," Alex said, feeling sweat break out under his collar.

"Yes, I think Lady Creighton, Miss Abingdon as she was then of course, introduced us." Mrs. Pembroke was watching him like a hawk.

She knows, Alex thought, his anger resurfacing. She and Marianne had been friends back then, had probably laughed over his infatuation. Had she egged Marianne on, urged her to agree to a secret engagement only to marry the wealthy Earl of Creighton a few weeks later?

"And have you and Lady Creighton remained close since?" he clipped out, reaching for his wine and draining it.

"Sadly, no. Her husband did not permit her to have friends."

Alex paused in the act of setting his glass down. "I beg your pardon?" he said, confused. "I never met the late Earl, but I heard stories of how he spoiled his wife, buying her more fashionable gowns and costly trinkets than any woman could want."

"If all a woman wanted were expensive baubles, indeed, Marianne was the luckiest woman in England," Mrs. Pembroke replied, and he heard the sarcasm in her voice. "Should she desire affection, respect, and the comfort of friendships, however, she was the veriest pauper."

That's what you get when you marry for mercenary motives, Alex wanted to snap back but forced himself to bite his tongue. Mrs. Pembroke was Marianne's partisan, which was useful information. He would ensure neither she nor her husband were available to intervene when he sought his private audience.

"I daresay being a rich widow will suit her a great deal better, in that case," he said caustically and nodded for the footman to top up his wine.

Chapter Ten

Marianne was acutely aware of Alexander watching her. Her hand shook as she tried to eat, and her voice sounded high and thin to her ears -- her laugh forced and artificial. Thomas looked quizzically at her once or twice, obviously picking up on her distress, but she refused to acknowledge his silent query, instead picking up her wine and drinking.

By the end of the meal, she realised what a mistake that was, however, since an attentive footman had kept her glass filled and she was more than a little tipsy. When Ellen invited the ladies to the parlour, it was more than enough reason to make her excuses and retire to bed.

"I have become unaccustomed to wine," she said quite truthfully, "and it has brought on my headache again. Please forgive me for retiring early; I promise I shall be more sociable tomorrow."

"You are forgiven already, though we shall miss your company. Sleep well and feel better, dearest, and please do not hesitate to have Jean or another maid bring you anything you might wish for your relief."

Marianne felt guilty about deceiving Ellen, but she lost no time in hurrying up the stairs, nervous all the while that Alexander might choose to leave the other men to their brandy and port and come looking for her. What he might have to say to her after all this time she could not imagine, but she knew she did not want to hear whatever it was. Merely looking on his face, only grown more handsome with the passage of years, was painful, especially since she'd had to listen to Lady Alleyne eagerly quizzing Lord Havers about Alexander's marriage prospects. He would need to marry, and soon; marquisates required heirs, and undoubtedly he would be choosing from among London's latest crop of debutantes.

Perhaps he even had someone in mind already. Miss Alleyne was a sweet creature with a hefty dowry; perhaps she might suit him. Or Lady Serena Thorpe; she would look very well on

Alexander's arm, and she had a strong character and a sense of humour too.

Marianne did not realise she was crying until she tripped, blinded by the tears in her eyes, and almost fell. Catching herself with a hand against the wall, she stumbled on until she found her room at last, pushing the door open with a sob of frustration when the knob stuck briefly.

"My lady!" Jean rose from where she had been seated by the fire mending a stocking, an expression of shock on her face as the sewing fell to the floor. "Are you unwell?"

"I feel sick," Marianne choked out, and Jean managed to get a pot under her nose just in time.

"That will teach me to drink too much wine," Marianne groaned a few minutes later, as Jean helped her to lie down and placed a cool, damp cloth over her brow. "Maybe my husband was right to insist I should only ever be permitted one glass."

"Well, it can be powerful stuff if you're not used to it," Jean agreed. "Especially if you don't eat nothin'."

Marianne's guilty silence made the maid sigh. But she hadn't been able to choke down more than a couple of spoonfuls of soup, not with the anger in Alexander's gaze scorching her from the other end of the table.

"I daresay you won't make the same mistake again, m'lady," Jean said, removing Marianne's slippers. "Let's get you comfortable for bed now, and I'll make a herbal tisane up for your head. A good night's sleep, and you'll be right as rain in the morning."

Privately, Marianne doubted she would sleep at all, but the tea Jean persuaded her to sip after helping her change into her night rail must have had some soothing herbs in it. Her eyelids soon began to feel heavy and she lay back against her pillows without complaint, allowing her eyes to close.

"That's it, m'lady," Jean encouraged softly, and Marianne heard her moving quietly about the room, setting things to rights and putting the noxious pot out for someone to take away and wash. "Sleep. You'll feel better in the morning."

Rejoining the ladies to discover Marianne had already retired infuriated Alexander to the point where he pleaded weariness from travelling and retired himself, ignoring Thomas' expression of disbelief. He was in no mood to be polite to anyone, and with no possible opportunity to corner Marianne tonight, he might as well retire rather than manage to offend one of the Havers' guests with his ill temper.

At the top of the stairs, he paused, considering briefly whether it might be worth trying to locate Marianne's room. His valet Simons would probably know exactly where everyone had been accommodated by now, and have opinions on whether Lady Havers had correctly placed them according to precedence, too. But asking Simons where he might find Lady Creighton's rooms and then going to look for the lady would create a scandal.

Alex did not care in the slightest if a scandal affected him, and Marianne deserved no consideration, but he would not see the Havers' first ever house party marred in such a way if he could help it. No, far better to bide his time and confront Marianne privately. One way or another, he would manage it.

And while he might not feel like company tonight, he had a good book to read, and undoubtedly Simons would be able to procure some of Havers' excellent brandy for him to drink while he did so.

Perhaps Simons might have some interesting gossip from belowstairs he could be convinced to share, as well. Marianne appeared to be well-settled here at Havers Hall; knowing how long she had been in residence and who was attending her could be useful information.

Making his way to the comfortable room he had been allotted on the second floor, Alex nodded to Simons as he entered. "I'm going to retire early, Simons; I'm in no mood for company."

"When are you ever, sir?" Simons rejoined smartly. "I took the liberty of obtaining some brandy for you." He indicated a decanter and glass sitting ready on the mantelpiece.

"In that case, you are forgiven for the snide remark on my social ineptitude." Alex threw himself into a seat by the fire.

"It's not your fault, sir," Simons said kindly. "The army didn't exactly provide you with many opportunities for civilised social interactions."

"Remind me again why I keep you around?" Alex asked dryly. For answer, Simons placed a glass of brandy into his hand, waved at his book placed ready for him on a table at his elbow, and indicated for him to lift his foot so Simons could start removing his boots. "Ah, yes. Of course. Because I couldn't do without you."

Simons gave a small smile and nodded before tugging his first boot off. "Did you enjoy your dinner, sir? I must say, the servants eat well here. I have rarely dined so heartily."

Embarrassed to admit he couldn't recall a single dish served that evening, Alex seized his opportunity gratefully. "Speaking of servants, Simons, who is attending Lady Creighton? I'm assuming she brought her own lady's maid, at least…"

"No, sir." Removing the other boot, Simons straightened up. "A maid named Jean has been assigned to her. A nice young woman and one not inclined to gossip about her mistress, even if it is only a temporary post for her. She was quite repressive when two of the other maids began to gossip about the unconventional manner in which the lady arrived."

"What unconventional manner?" Alex looked up.

"That I have not yet been able to discern, sir. So far, all I know is that she arrived a full week earlier than expected." Simons hesitated. "May I enquire as to your interest in Lady Creighton, sir?"

"No."

"Very good, sir. I shall see what further information I may glean tomorrow." Simons knew better than to press when Alex spoke in that flat tone; the valet removed himself, taking Alex's boots through to his adjoining chamber where he would polish them to a high shine.

113

Left alone, Alex brooded over his brandy, staring into the glowing coals of the fire. Why had Marianne come a week early, and under what 'unconventional' circumstances? Perhaps she had been escorted by a man, he thought suddenly; that would certainly be unconventional. She was a very beautiful widow, after all. Perhaps a lover had brought her here - cast her off? That would explain her arrival a week early, too.

By the time he'd finished the second glass of brandy, Alex had convinced himself his theory was correct. Which meant Marianne would be looking for a new lover.

A wolfish smile curved his lips as he drained the glass and set it down.

That was a role he'd gladly fulfil for her.

Waking early the following morning, Alex could not remember the last time he'd slept so well. He could not recall the last time he retired so early, either; perhaps that had something to do with getting a good night's sleep, he acknowledged with a grin at his own foolishness.

Simons bustled about importantly, bringing him riding clothes and suggesting he might wish to go for an early ride, as rain was expected later in the day.

114

"Julius will want a run," Alex agreed, accepting his gloves from the valet. "And I daresay breakfast will be served throughout the morning, at the convenience of guests?"

"Indeed, sir. There is a morning room in the east wing where a buffet will be kept ready until noon, I understand. Any of the house servants can escort you there."

Perhaps I'll catch Marianne there. Or perhaps she will be out riding herself, Alex thought as he headed downstairs and out to the stables, spying a lady by the mounting-block being assisted up onto a pretty dappled grey mare. As he drew closer, however, he recognised Ellen, Thomas waiting to one side, already mounted on a leggy chestnut gelding.

"Good morning!" Ellen called to him in delight as she saw him approaching. "It is a lovely morning for a ride; would you care to accompany us?"

Alex acknowledged it was indeed a fine morning, especially for December; the air was crisp and clear, frost riming the grass, a light breeze blowing. He could hardly decline the invitation, either, though he remarked that his horse would want a good gallop.

115

"We can certainly accommodate that," Thomas said cheerfully. "I saw your stallion; he's a fine fellow. John Pembroke will want to talk with you about maybe taking him down to Hampshire to visit with some of his mares, I daresay."

"No doubt Julius would enjoy the holiday." Alex winked cheekily at Ellen. "Especially with eager ladies waiting for him at the end of the trip!"

Ellen blushed a little. "Outrageous, Glenkellie," she reproved. "Apparently you have forgotten, in your years in the army, that *true* ladies do not appreciate bawdy talk." Her eyes twinkled, though, and Alex knew she'd already forgiven him.

"Forgive me, Lady Havers." He executed a bow to her. "I shall endeavour to remember my manners."

Julius was led out then by a groom; Alex greeted the stallion fondly. The former warhorse nickered and pushed his head against Alex's chest, sending him back an involuntary step with the force of the shove.

"Behave, you great fool," Alex said in amusement, fishing an apple from his pocket.

"He truly is beautiful," Ellen commented as Alex mounted up and rode up alongside her. "What colour is that called? His body looks almost blue, though his head and legs are black."

"That's what it's called, blue roan. It's a trick of the light; the individual hairs are black and white, evenly mixed." Alex patted Julius' thickly muscled neck affectionately. "He carried me through many a battle in Belgium and France. Frankly, he's earned a quiet retirement and as many lady friends as he wishes."

"If only all England's valiant soldiers could have the same," Ellen said sincerely.

Touched, Alex bowed to her again. Julius frisked a few steps as his weight shifted, and Alex reined him in firmly. "Not yet, boy. Not yet."

"Not so fast as a thoroughbred, I daresay, but unstoppable once you get him up to speed?" Thomas asked, reining in his chestnut on Ellen's other side.

"Quite so," Alex agreed. "Thoroughbreds are all very well for racing a mile or so, but for long campaigns and cavalry charges, a stronger and more durable mount is needed. Your mount might win a short race, but over the course of a day, Julius would run him into the ground." He patted the charger's proudly arched neck.

"Well, we haven't a day," Thomas said, "so we can only challenge you to a short race, I'm afraid."

"We?" Alex queried.

"Watch out for Lady Havers. She races to win," Thomas said with a grin, and was proved right a moment later as Ellen urged her mare to a gallop, shouting over her shoulder;

"Last one to the split oak is a rotten egg!"

Laughing, Alex gave Julius his head, and in the stallion's joyous gallop of freedom forgot for a little while all the concerns which plagued his restless mind.

Chapter Eleven

From the windows of the morning room, Marianne watched the three riders as they crossed the landscape into the distance. Alexander was unmistakable, tall and straight-backed; he sat his horse with the ease of someone who had lived in his saddle for nearly months on end.

"Lady Creighton."

A voice behind her made her turn, and she smiled as she saw Amelia Pembroke. "Please, call me Marianne," she invited. "I would as soon forget my marriage ever happened, to tell the truth."

They were alone save for a couple of servants bustling about the buffet laid out on a dresser at the other end of the room, and Amelia gave her a sympathetic look. "I can quite understand why you feel that way. I never told you before, but I was so

119

very shocked when your engagement was announced and then you married Creighton so quickly. I thought you'd have eloped with Rotherhithe before marrying a man you didn't love."

"Had he given me the opportunity, I would have done." Marianne looked back to the window. The three horses were galloping now, dwindling to specks before fading from sight entirely, swallowed up by a fold of the landscape. "He had already taken ship for the Peninsula, though. The marriage had no doubt already taken place by the time he could even have heard of the engagement, but I still hoped he would do something - come back and challenge Creighton, shoot him dead, and take me away."

Amelia said nothing, but her look spoke volumes of understanding.

"I was very young."

"Do you hold any hopes in Rotherhithe - excuse me, he's Glenkellie now, of course - any hopes in his direction?"

"Good Lord, no." Marianne willed her hand not to shake as she cut her toast into small, delicate triangles. "It's long in the past, Amelia. We've both moved on. He needs a wealthy, well-connected young bride to produce the next generation of

Rotherhithes, not a barren, penniless widow who is all but cast-off from her family!"

"I beg your pardon." Amelia blinked.

Marianne realised the other woman did not know of her full situation. "I'm afraid Creighton was as callous in death as in life," she said ruefully, before quietly explaining the terms of her dower and her falling-out with Arthur and Lavinia.

"How *appalling*," Amelia said with her usual forthrightness once Marianne had finished speaking. "I don't know which I find worse; that Creighton treated you so shabbily, or that his heir seeks to compound the insult!"

Marianne smiled wryly but said nothing as a footman set a steaming teapot and a polished wooden tea caddy down on the table between them. Opening the caddy, she spooned some of the fragrant leaves into the hot water.

"Considering my husband's character, I should have expected no less," she said finally.

"Well, I think it's disgraceful," Amelia said hotly, "and I should like to extend an invitation to you to come to Hampshire and live with us, as my dear friend, once you are weary of London. You need only send a note and I will have Pembroke come himself with a carriage to collect you." She smiled a little shyly and leaned close. "I shall want a friend close by in a few months," she confided. "I am enceinte, at last."

"That is wonderful news and a most generous offer," Marianne said warmly. "I thank you for it most gratefully. I daresay I will spend the rest of my days imposing on all of my friends in turn until they are all heartily sick of me darkening their doors!"

"Never," Amelia disclaimed loyally.

They were joined then by the Alleyne family, who came in en masse, exclaiming excitedly over how well they had slept, how comfortable the beds were, and how attentive the servants of Havers Hall. Marianne was not displeased to end her conversation with Amelia; discussing her future prospects was a depressing topic indeed, though it warmed her heart to know she still had Amelia's friendship.

They were still at table when the riders returned; Amelia's husband had met up with the others out in the countryside somewhere and the four entered the morning room with broad smiles and hearty appetites. Tempted to excuse herself immediately, Marianne realised it would be rather rude as Mr. Pembroke took a seat by his wife and leaned across her to bid Marianne a cheerful good morning.

"It is indeed, sir. Did you enjoy your ride?"

"Very much so; it is a fine morning for a hearty gallop!" He turned to his wife. "I am sorry you were not feeling well enough to join me, my heart," he said in an undertone, picking up Amelia's hand and kissing it. "Are you quite recovered?"

"I am." Amelia smiled fondly at him. "I have invited Marianne to come stay with us, perhaps in early May or so."

"Ah." Mr. Pembroke glanced at Marianne before looking back at his wife, who nodded at him. "Lady Creighton would be most welcome at any time, but if you would like her with you then, I shall move heaven and earth to find some way to persuade her."

"Such efforts will not be required, I promise." Marianne gave him a warm smile. "I am delighted to accept the invitation and may only need to impose on you for some transport, probably from London."

"It is not the slightest imposition, my lady." Pembroke dismissed her concerns with a wave of his hand.

Boots on the polished wooden floorboards heralded another arrival, and Marianne glanced up, only to meet Alexander's eyes as he entered the room.

Catherine Bilson

All the breath seemed to rush out of her body, and she clenched her hands tightly in her lap, digging her nails into her palms.

Steady. Steady, she ordered herself. *It was all a long time ago. Alexander is nothing to you now.*

The pounding of her heart told her she was a liar - and the look of scorn on Alexander's face told her there was nothing she could do to turn back the clock, anyway. Lowering her eyes, she tried to take slow, calming breaths and regain her composure.

Breakfast seemed to last an unconscionably long time, with everyone chatting sociably about their plans for the day. Though he'd worked up a hearty appetite on the ride, the food tasted like ashes to Alexander.

Look at her, sitting among decent folk, acting as though she hasn't a care in the world.

Every smile Marianne offered someone else was like a dagger to his chest. Viscount Thorpington -- seated directly opposite her -- kept missing his mouth with his fork as he gazed at her, utterly entranced, and young Joseph Alleyne was no better. Alexander's hand clenched around his knife until his knuckles turned white; he didn't notice how tight his grip was until his fingers began to cramp painfully.

"Is your beefsteak not to your liking, Glenkellie?" Thomas enquired politely as Alex dropped the knife with a clatter.

"It's fine, thank you," Alex muttered, massaging his stiff fingers. "A sudden cramp, that's all."

Thomas gave him a sceptical look before his gaze moved to where Marianne sat. "Is that what you call it?"

A dull flush suffused Alex's cheeks, and he looked away, picking his knife up and cutting into his steak again. Fortunately, Sir Tobias Alleyne leaned over to speak to Thomas, saving Alex from having to think up a response to the awkward question.

The ladies began to drift away from the table first, Ellen announcing they would be gathering in the front parlour to converse. "I regret I have no particular activities planned for the day, but with the rest of the guests due to arrive I must be here to welcome them," she said, and at once the other ladies were declaring they should like nothing better than a relaxing morning sitting in a comfortable parlour with a warm fire.

"Don't forget your embroidery, dear," Lady Alleyne told her daughter, who sighed. Marianne sympathised. She had always found embroidery deadly dull, too.

"Or, should you prefer, Havers Hall has a wonderful library," she said confidingly to Miss Alleyne, "which they are most obliging about letting one browse. Would you like to come and look for something to read with me?"

"Very much!" Miss Alleyne said quickly before her mother could object, and Lady Serena promptly asked if she might come with them too.

Marianne led the two young women off to the library, smiling with pleasure as they both exclaimed over the collection. Leaving them considering the choices from a shelf of novels, she browsed deeper into the stacks, recalling she had spied some travelogues last time she'd visited the room. Stories of exotic lands and adventurous (if probably highly fictionalised) derring-do might be just the thing to keep her mind occupied.

Sitting down by a window to leaf through a book about an intrepid Englishwoman's travels in the Orient, Marianne lost track of time. She did not hear the two younger women come to the end of the row of shelves where she sat, did not see the amused glance they traded before they stole away quietly, leaving her quite alone.

She almost jumped out of her skin, however, when a deep voice said, "So *this* is where you're hiding."

Marianne clenched her hands on the book, trying to hide their trembling, and took a moment to compose herself before she looked up. "Hiding? Hardly," she said, trying to keep her tone light and amused. "I'm sure I was quite clear in declaring my intentions to come here. After all, it wasn't difficult for you to find me, was it, Lord Glenkellie?"

Alexander stared down at her, his eyes hard and cold like chips of ice. A tic made the scar on his cheek jump like a living thing as he clenched his jaw. Then he surprised her again by taking a seat on the window seat next to her. Too close! His thigh, muscled and hard beneath tight nankeen breeches, was pressed against hers through the woollen fabric of her skirt. Marianne tried to shift away, but she'd used the wall at her side to lean on when she took her seat and there was little room to move.

"We need to talk," he said finally.

"About what?" She genuinely couldn't imagine what he might have to say to her after all these years.

"I know what you're up to."

Marianne blinked, confused, and stopped trying to avoid Alexander's eyes. "I beg your pardon?"

"Leave Thorpington and Alleyne out of your schemes. They're nice young men who deserve better than to have their hearts broken just because you're bored."

"I *beg* your pardon!" Her mouth fell open with shock.

"You're repeating yourself, and you understand me quite well, I believe. Don't encourage those two boys - or you'll answer to me."

Marianne's cheeks flushed with sudden fury. "I do not care for your insinuations, and allow me to make it clear that I do not answer to you on any matter, Lord Glenkellie!" She made to rise, but a powerful hand closed around her wrist, holding her firmly in place.

"Not so fast, *my lady*." His deep voice put a mocking inflection on her title.

"Unhand me at once!" Her gaze spat daggers as she looked at him, her voice cold and brittle as ice. She was still surprised when he let go, his large fingers opening quickly.

"Your pardon," he mumbled, flushing darkly. "I did not intend - I have never laid hand to a woman in anger before."

"Then what in heaven's name possessed you to do so now?" Marianne demanded, her anger fuelling her tongue. "What have I ever done to you, that you should raise your hand to *me*?"

Alexander stared at her in silence.

Disgusted, she rose and tried to leave, but as she reached the end of the row of shelves, four quiet words stopped her in her tracks.

"You broke my heart."

Chapter Twelve

Alexander didn't know what made him confess it. Perhaps it had been Marianne's righteous fury after he grabbed her arm, tried to force her to listen. He was still shocked at himself for behaving that way; he had been raised to believe violence against women was utterly beyond the bounds of civilised behaviour.

Marianne's face, as she turned slowly back to face him, was hard to read. She had paled from her flushed rage, but he realised when she spoke that she was no less furious.

"Do you think I *willingly* married a man more than three times my age?"

Opening his mouth to answer in the affirmative, Alex saw the glint of fury in her eyes and closed it again.

"Oh, I see." Her voice softened and she looked truly disappointed. "You never knew me at all, did you? What did you think, that I led you on for my own amusement and then married the richest man I could catch?"

He couldn't remember feeling so small since he was six years old and summoned to meet his grandfather for the first time. The old man's piercing gaze had stripped him to the bone, and he felt just as flayed by the beautiful woman standing in front of him now, shaking her head slowly over his arrogant assumptions.

To his surprise, Marianne returned to sit down, though she moved to the other side of the window seat, leaving a full foot of space between them.

"For the sake of the affection we once held each other in," she said, "and because I believe you when you say I broke your heart, I pray you will allow me to tell you the truth about my marriage to Creighton."

Childishly, he didn't want to hear it. If she was telling the truth, it meant his resentment of her, his unkind thoughts about her, were wrong. That *he* was wrong. It was an unpalatable truth for any man to bear, but particularly one of his rank and his military experience. In all those years on the battlefield, his instincts had never led him astray.

Yet now…

"I hated him." Marianne's voice made him look up at her and meet her eyes despite the guilt which made him want to study his shoes. If she was willing to speak of something which must have been deeply unpleasant, at the very least he owed her the courtesy of listening.

"From the moment I first laid eyes on Creighton, I disliked him. He licked his lips when he spoke to me and looked on me as though I was a possession to be owned -- a *thing* he coveted. My father's gambling debts made it an easy transaction; I was bought and sold with the handing over of a bank draft. Like a piece of livestock, or an ornamental vase."

Alex felt vaguely sick. Marianne showed no emotion as she spoke, merely reciting the facts in a flat tone, despite the ugliness of the circumstances she related.

"Though I objected vociferously when the engagement announcement appeared in the newspapers, my opinion was not sought and my consent not required. Indeed, when I was summoned to my father's study one morning, I had not the slightest idea I was going to my own wedding. With a special licence in hand and a vicar who did not care in the slightest about my protestations, Creighton made me his countess."

"Marianne," Alex said, his voice choked, "please... don't."

"Don't what?" Her tone hardened, her fists clenching against her skirts. "Don't tell you about the way two of his footmen forced me upstairs to a guest suite *in my own home* where my husband of but half an hour raped me with my father's full approval? Of the many indignities I suffered at Creighton's hands -- most particularly every month when my courses came and he would beat me for not conceiving an heir?" There were tears in her eyes, and Alexander hated himself for making her relive the memories which obviously caused her such pain.

"Christ!" Alex couldn't sit still any longer. Erupting to his feet, he ran his hands through his hair, tugging at the strands in frustration. If Creighton was still alive, he'd challenge and shoot the bastard himself, but there was no one to take his anger out on. "Marianne... I'm sorry. I'm sorry that happened to you, and I'm sorry I thought the worst of you. *I'm sorry.*"

She sat with her hands folded primly in her lap now, gazing up at him from her blue eyes, looking like a perfect porcelain doll. Finally she inclined her head a fraction. "We have both been at war," she said, her voice softer now. One delicate hand lifted, gesturing towards his face. "You merely have a more visible scar than I, that is all."

An hour ago, he would have become enraged hearing anyone claim any experience might compare to the battles he had endured, the awful things he had seen in the war. Now, after hearing Marianne's unemotional recital, he knew better. "At least I had days and even weeks where there was quiet and peace," he said. "Your battles were fought every night."

"And every day," she corrected with a twisted little smile. "I was constantly on display as Creighton's most prized possession, you see, and God help me if I allowed so much as a hair to stray out of place."

His voice shook as he asked "Did he beat you?" He had no right to the answer and said so immediately after he asked the question, wishing he could take it back. He'd made her suffer enough reliving the memories she'd already shared with him.

"Yes," she answered him anyway. "Until his arm grew too weak to inflict enough pain to make me cry out, that is. Or perhaps, I just became inured to it." She paused a moment, looking down at her hands. Her fingers clenched again, knuckles showing white, before she deliberately relaxed them to smooth at her skirt. "At any rate, then he had one of his footmen take over, a burly fellow named Stokes who seemed to take a good deal of pleasure in making me scream."

Alex's fists clenched. He could at least hunt down Stokes and make him see the error of his ways - but Marianne leaned forward and placed her hand on one of his.

"Revenge should have no bounds, as the Bard said, and I took mine. Perhaps making a false accusation is a sin, but I took a good deal of pleasure in accusing Stokes of stealing some of Creighton's belongings a few days after his death. The Earl of Havers was of much assistance to me in having him taken up for theft. He has been transported to Botany Bay, I understand."

"That's not enough punishment," Alex growled.

"It is enough for me." Marianne looked surprisingly serene as she lifted her hand from his and sat back against the window. "Creighton is dead. He no longer has the power to harm me."

"Yet you still bear his name; does that not grieve you?"

"Of course it does." She smiled wryly. "It is why I encourage my friends to call me Marianne, and why I seek to make friends with new people as quickly as possible. I would far rather throw out propriety and go only by my first name; if I could, I would never hear the name of Creighton again."

"You could remarry?" Alex suggested, suddenly wondering what her opinion was on the subject.

She laughed, throaty and full. "You jest! Willingly put myself once again under the power of a man who can do whatever he wishes to me and never suffer the slightest consequence for it? No thank you." Standing, she smoothed her skirts. "Thank you for hearing me out, Lord Glenkellie. I once held you in a good deal of affection, and though you had every right to despise me for jilting you without warning, it grieved me to discover you held such a low opinion of me. I hope you understand me a little better now."

"You have held up a mirror and shown me the ugliness in my own soul," Alex said, "and I hope you will call me Alexander or merely Glenkellie, and permit me the use of your given name should we again have occasion to converse privately. In any case, I vow the name your husband inflicted on you against your will shall never pass my lips again in your hearing; henceforth in public you shall be *Lady Marianne* to me."

"I am not entitled to that, I'm afraid. I am only a viscount's daughter, after all."

Alex found a small smile despite his inner turmoil, hoping to amuse her with his next remark. "One benefit of being a marquis, I have found, is that very few people dare to correct you. I need only declare I am confusing you with the current Countess and you will soon find half London is giving you the honorary elevation."

Her lips twitched, and he thought she might, indeed, be slightly amused. "As you please, Glenkellie. I learned well the advantages of high rank in setting trends among the Ton. If you wish to use yours to my benefit, I shall not protest."

"It's the least I can do." He executed a deep bow, far deeper than mere courtesy called for. "If I may be of service in any other way, I hope you will not hesitate to call on me."

"Thank you." She curtseyed in return, and then said, "It is possible I may take you up on that offer, Glenkellie."

"It would be my honour to assist, Lady Marianne."

Inclining her head, she turned and walked away, leaving Alex pacing, furious with himself.

What a pig he'd been, making assumptions of the basest kind with not the slightest evidence to support them! And what poor Marianne had suffered! Watching her leave, the skirts of her plain dark grey woollen gown swaying slightly as she moved, he realised she was almost certainly wearing such a plain garment to avoid attracting the attention of men. Perhaps, because of the way Creighton had demanded she display herself, garbed in the finest gowns and jewels -- always a perfect fashion plate -- wearing such a dowdy dress now was a form of rebellion.

Eventually, his anger at himself cooled somewhat, Alex left the library and proceeded downstairs.

"Lord Glenkellie." The butler, Allsopp, intercepted him in the front hall. "May I direct you anywhere? The other gentlemen are in the billiard room."

"Thank you, Allsopp," he said gruffly, "but I am in no mood for company. I might take a walk down to the stables, see that my horse is behaving himself for the grooms here."

"Very good, my lord," Allsopp said, unruffled. "Allow me to fetch your hat and greatcoat."

Impatient with the delay, Alex nonetheless stayed long enough to don the coat and hat which were swiftly produced. It was getting cold outside, and he thought the forecasted rain was likely to begin soon. Walking briskly to the stables, the chill air helped to cool the rage still boiling in his blood. By the time he found Julius settled in a large, comfortable stable with knee-deep straw to lie down in, a manger full of hay, and a bucket full of fresh water, he felt almost normal again. Rubbing the stallion's ears, he murmured nonsense to him and was glad the sensitive horse did not pick up on his mood.

The Havers stable is exceptional, Alex noted as he looked around at contented horses in their stalls and stable lads busily polishing tack or scrubbing out used feed buckets. He need have no concerns for his horses here.

A coach rolled into the yard as he exited the stable, and he sighed.

"More new arrivals? Who are these?" he asked the head stableman, who came out to look.

"Oh no, not this coach, my lord. This is the one m'lord Havers sent to Cumbria to collect the Lady Creighton's belongings."

"I beg your pardon?" Alex said, startled, but the man had already hurried away, going to take the heads of the lead pair.

That made no sense. *Why hadn't Marianne travelled with her belongings? Why would Thomas have had to send for them?* Perhaps this was the 'odd circumstances' surrounding her arrival Simons had heard about. Alex determined immediately to set his valet to further investigation. He'd learned his lesson; he would make no further assumptions about Marianne without being in full possession of the facts, he was determined.

Chapter Thirteen

Heart still beating fast as she hurried away from the library, Marianne paused at the parlour door for only a moment before turning away and stealing up the stairs. Allsopp pretended not to see her as she scurried past him, and she shot the butler a grateful look, knowing the apparently crusty exterior hid a kindly heart. He would disclaim knowledge of her to anyone who enquired, she was sure, though she would hardly be difficult to find.

Her rooms were empty when she entered, Jean obviously gone on some errand; not that Marianne cared. Right now, she wanted nothing more than quiet and solitude to think over the astonishing conversation she'd just had with Alexander. He'd obviously thought the worst of her, which was truly disheartening. But then, if she really had broken his heart all those years ago, she supposed he had a right to feel angry. *The most surprising thing*, Marianne mused as she curled up in the comfortable chair by the fire, kicked off her slippers, and tucked her feet under her, *was Alexander's evident fury when I told him of my ill-treatment at Creighton's hands. It's almost as though he still had feelings for me.* She had more than half-expected him not to believe her, to accuse her of making it up. Yet he had listened without interruption, and shown a deepening expression of commingled horror and rage. He really had believed her.

Marianne could not quite comprehend what on earth had made her tell Alexander so much. She had never spoken the whole sordid truth of her marriage to anyone, had never planned to do so. But when she'd discovered he'd thought she had married Creighton willingly, the words had just exploded out of her, and once she started she could not seem to stop until she had told him the worst of it, though not all -- that would have taken days to tell, and she did not care to dwell on all she had suffered. Now she felt curiously light, as though by sharing the truth with ALexander she had purged a dark weight from herself.

Knowing Alexander condemned Creighton's actions was pleasing, too, even if his suggestion she should marry again was laughable. Men who showed a kindly face to the outside world could be monsters behind closed doors. Creighton had publicly played a devoted husband who enjoyed showering his beautiful young wife with gifts, after all. How many ladies had expressed their envy, declared their wishes their husbands would be so generous?

Shuddering at the memory of the price she had paid for Creighton's generosity, Marianne's attention was caught by the sound of hooves on the avenue's gravel-strewn path. Peering from her window, she saw a plain dark coach rolling towards the house, drawn by four horses, unmatched in colour but sturdy-looking. Wondering if she should go down to join Ellen and the others to greet new arrivals, she frowned curiously as the coach did not pull up at the front door but rolled around the side of the house beyond her view. *Perhaps some servants arriving ahead of their employers*, she finally guessed, and returned to her own musings.

Alexander's offer of help if she should ever require it had been most unexpected, but not unwelcome. Indeed, she honestly believed he meant it - and considering the uncertainty of her future, it was very possible she might one day need to ask for his aid in some manner. She would never ask for financial assistance, of course, but as a marquis there were many things he could accomplish with a mere snap of his fingers which would be utterly impossible for her to achieve.

Hasty footsteps outside her room made her look up, and then the door opened.

"Oh, my lady!" Startled, Jean dropped a curtsey. "I do beg your pardon; I thought you were downstairs with the other ladies!"

"It's quite all right, Jean. I just wanted a little solitude, that's all. No, no, it's fine; do come on in." Slipping her feet from under her, Marianne rose.

"It's just that your things have arrived, my lady!" Jean exclaimed. "All the way from Cumbria!"

"Oh!" Startled, Marianne watched as Jean moved aside to let a small procession of footmen enter the room, carrying an apparently unending stream of trunks and packages. "Did they bring my *whole* wardrobe?" she asked, startled.

"M'lord earl sent his steward with instructions that anything which belonged to you must be packed," one of the footmen said with a bow in her direction. "Sent all Lady Havers' trunks for them to be packed in, too."

"Oh, how very kind!" It would have been of no consequence to Thomas, she knew, but it made all the difference to her to have all her own gowns and belongings. Two more maids arrived to help Jean unpack as the footmen filed out. Marianne joined her maids, exclaiming with pleasure as the trunks were thrown open to reveal silks and satins in every colour of the rainbow.

"There's a letter in this one, m'lady," one of the maids said, holding out a folded paper.

Marianne accepted it, moving out of the way as the maids continued unpacking efficiently. *Aunt Marianne* was written on the outside in a neat, precise hand, and she smiled as she returned to her chair to open it. Either Diana or Clarissa, she guessed, had written the note.

Dear Aunt Marianne, I kept the two dresses you gave to me, and Clarissa entirely filled her work box with ribbons and lace, but we helped the maids pack everything else from your wardrobe. Papa did not want to open his strongbox to hand over the jewels the previous Earl bought you, but Lord Havers' steward was quite insistent. We hope you are well and enjoying your stay with your friends and anticipate eagerly seeing you in London in the New Year, as Mama and Papa are now quite resigned the whole family must go. With love, Diana.

A knock on the door startled Marianne, and Jean left the unpacking to scurry over and open it. "M'lord Havers for you, my lady," she advised Marianne.

"Thank you." Tucking the note into her pocket, Marianne pushed her feet into her slippers and went to the door.

"My lady." Thomas tipped his head respectfully. "I wonder if you would grant me a few minutes of your time, in my study perhaps?"

"Certainly." Nodding to Jean to continue her work, Marianne left her room and fell into step beside Thomas. He offered his arm gallantly, and she accepted with a smile.

"Jean is taking care of you to your satisfaction, I hope?" he enquired.

"She is by far the most obliging maid I have ever had," Marianne said honestly, "and I would be delighted to write her an excellent reference at any time in the future, should she require one."

"I think she was rather hoping you might offer her a permanent post in your service, actually," Thomas remarked.

"I only wish I could. Without a fixed income, though, I fear I could not guarantee her long-term employment, and it would be quite unfair to Jean."

"As to that," Thomas said as they turned to descend the stairs together, "I have some ideas which could provide quite a nice little income for you, with a small initial investment."

"Yet I have no money to invest, Thomas!" She cast a despairing look up at him. "Have you forgotten already how I arrived on your doorstep? Surely not, since your men have just returned from collecting the belongings I was unable to bring with me, for which I cannot thank you enough!"

Thomas made a negating gesture. "Do not think on it. You befriended Ellen in London when she was a wallflower, and I can never sufficiently express to you my gratitude for that kindness."

"I have never been more glad of the impulse which drove me to speak to her that night," Marianne insisted, "for I have found the sister I always wished I had."

"She says the same of you, and I consider you my own sister as well," Thomas said, "which is why I am happy to perform any service within my power."

They had arrived at the study, and Thomas opened the door to usher Marianne inside. A large wooden box was sitting in the middle of the desk, a sheaf of paper beside it.

"Please." Thomas showed Marianne to a chair, and she sat down, looking curiously at Thomas as he gathered the papers up. "Apparently, your late husband kept records of all the jewellery pieces he purchased for you."

"Well, yes, but I understood they were all estate property and had now passed to the new Lady Creighton," Marianne said, startled.

"Had he recorded the purchases differently, perhaps they might have, but when his solicitors visited the bank while probating the estate, the jewels were each stored with the purchase receipts, copies of which you see here." Thomas offered her the sheaf of papers. "Each of them has a handwritten note at the bottom which reads, 'Purchased for Marianne'."

Even the sight of her former husband's handwriting, large and spiky, the pen almost stabbing through the page, sent a shiver down Marianne's spine. She glanced only at the top sheet before asking, "I don't understand what that means, I'm sorry. Surely if they were purchased with Creighton money, they still belong to the estate?"

"Under the law, they belong to you. I suspected such was the case; on the last occasion I spoke with the former Earl, he showed me a pearl brooch he had ordered for you, and I saw the receipt with that exact note on it. When I wrote to the current Earl requesting he send your belongings back with my men, I noted it would be simpler for him to send the jewels with my steward rather than me having to contact his solicitors to request their return on your behalf."

She remembered that pearl brooch. Creighton had given it to her the day before Thomas and Ellen's wedding and all but commanded her to wear it. An ugly, gaudy thing guaranteed to draw the eye, she had done her best to conceal it by pinning it at her waist rather than to her bosom. She half-thought it had been Creighton's anger over her defiance, small as it had been, which had led to his fatal apoplexy, though it could have been any number of small transgressions on her part. She'd been enjoying herself that day, after all.

"I don't want it," she said instinctively as Thomas handed her a small iron key and nodded towards the chest.

"The brooch?"

"Any of it." Putting the key down on the desk, Marianne shook her head. "This is the only jewellery I have ever cared to wear." She reached to her throat, where a simple silver cross hung on a fine chain. "It was my mother's, the only thing I have left of her. My father sold her other jewels to fund his gambling, but this wasn't worth enough for him to bother with. Creighton never permitted me to wear it; now that I have the choice, I would as soon not wear anything else."

"Quite understandable," Thomas said kindly. "In which case, why not consider selling them? Some of these pieces are worth a considerable sum, you know."

"They are?" Marianne had never thought on it. Creighton had never permitted her to see bills or receipts for anything; her accounts were all sent directly to him.

"Certainly according to these. Three hundred and seventy-five pounds for a ruby necklace and ear bobs, for example."

Marianne frowned. "A ruby necklace? I never had a ruby necklace."

"Purchased from Garrard's a few days before his passing. It's possible he never got the chance to present it to you." Picking up the key she had rejected, Thomas opened the box, checked a number on one of the papers, and took out a flat jewel case with a number written in chalk on the lid.

"Ugh," Marianne grumbled when Thomas opened the box. The necklace was gaudy in the extreme, the ear bobs heavy-looking. "I would have hated to wear that."

"Well, if I were going to spend several hundred pounds at Garrard's, I don't think that's what I'd have chosen," Thomas said diplomatically.

Reaching out to close the box, Marianne shook her head. "Even if he had better taste, I should still not wish to wear jewels he chose for me. At least I was permitted to choose my own gowns, even if they always had to be in the first stare of fashion. These… were a demonstration of his power over me, nothing more. I don't want them."

"So let us arrange to sell them," Thomas said practically. "If we are able to achieve prices even half what Creighton paid, you will have a nice little nest egg. Look on it as a proper widow's jointure, if you will."

"I shall indeed," she decided, pleased at the notion of disposing of the jewels and gaining a measure of financial independence at the same time. "Would you assist me with the sale, Thomas? I would not know where to begin."

"Neither do I, but I will investigate on your behalf how to achieve the best prices, I promise you."

"Perhaps Lord Glenkellie might assist?" she offered tentatively, knowing Alexander knew far more people in London than Thomas.

Thomas gave her a curious look. "I was under the impression you and Glenkellie weren't on the best of terms," he said cautiously.

"A misunderstanding," Marianne prevaricated, "and one which is now in the past. I believe he would be amenable to providing some contacts, at least."

"Then I shall ask his assistance. In the meantime, would you like me to have the box placed in your room?"

"No," she said immediately. "Just... lock it up somewhere safe, if you please."

"Whatever you wish."

She blessed Thomas for not asking any more questions. He had a very good idea how miserable her marriage had been, she suspected, though she had shared far fewer details with him and Ellen than with Alexander.

Instead, he only replaced the ruby necklace in the box, locked it up again, and handed her a single sheet of paper, saying that was the complete inventory of the box's contents. Written by his steward, it had been countersigned by Arthur, certifying all the jewels belonged to her, Marianne, and were not the property of the Creighton estate. There were far more than she'd realised, and the total at the bottom of the sheet made her eyes pop. Thomas was quite right; if they were able to achieve prices even half the new sale value of the jewels, financial independence truly would be within her grasp.

Chapter Fourteen

The jewels could be the answer to my money problems, Marianne thought as she folded the paper and put it in her pocket alongside Diana's note. Climbing the stairs to return to her room, she mused on the possibilities. She would be able to offer Jean a position. She could buy a cottage somewhere for the two of them, but retiring to a country cottage didn't appeal. Better to invest the money, with Thomas' advice, and stick with her original plan of spending most of the year staying with friends. At least she would be able to pay her own way now without being entirely dependent on the generosity of others, which was a huge relief.

"My lady." Jean turned to her, face aglow, when Marianne re-entered her room. "I have never seen such gowns!"

The maid was holding a gown in her hands, one Marianne vaguely recalled ordering and not yet wearing. Made of a dark emerald silk, it had delicate gold embroidery all over the bodice and around the hem and cuffs.

"Such *fabric*," Jean said almost reverently. "It isn't even crushed!"

"That's good silk for you," Marianne said with a nod. "I'd forgotten how beautiful this was." Fingering the sleeve, she asked, "Shall I wear it tonight, do you think?"

"Oh, yes!" Jean cried enthusiastically. "I cannot imagine any colour better suited to you, my lady; you will be the focus of all eyes!"

"You flatter me, but I am also convinced." Marianne hesitated before saying, "I know you already helped me dress once today, Jean, but now that my better gowns are here I believe I should like to change out of the one I am wearing. I've been rotating the same two gowns for almost a fortnight now."

"Of course, my lady." Reverently laying the emerald silk on the bed, Jean hurried into the dressing room, where the other two maids were still unpacking trunks and hanging gowns. "How about this one, my lady?"

The gown was wool instead of silk, but a fine, soft lambswool dyed to a lovely shade of gentian blue-violet. Beautifully cut, Marianne recalled it to be both warm and comfortable to wear.

"Perfect," she said, pleased by Jean's choice, and stood still to let her maid help with her buttons.

Changed into a fine gown, Marianne began to feel a little of her old confidence returning. She had always moved with ease among the highest of high society, she recalled, uncaring of what any of them thought of her. Their opinions had no power to harm her, after all, and facing very real threats every day of her marriage had inured her to petty insult. Her apparent fearlessness had made her surprisingly popular among the highest sticklers including the patronesses at Almack's.

Recalling how she had faced down a Russian princess and any number of duchesses, countesses, and more without fear made Marianne smile as she smoothed her hands over her skirts. Her fine gowns were just as much armour as any medieval knight's plate and shield.

"Oh, you've something in your pocket, my lady." Jean held out the folded sheets of paper she'd discovered in the pocket of the discarded gown. "Would you like them with you, or should I put them in the writing-desk?"

Thinking she should write a letter to Diana thanking her and telling her the expected date of the Havers party's arrival in London, Marianne nodded. "In the writing-desk, thank you, Jean."

"Very good, my lady. What shoes will you wear?"

"Oh, these slippers will be fine." Marianne glanced down at the tan kidskin slippers she had been wearing all morning. Jean looked a little disapproving, but Marianne was unmoved. She'd brought those slippers with her because they were her favourites, snug and comfortable on her feet. It wasn't as though anyone would see more than the tips of her toes below her gown's long skirt.

Garbed in a fresh, high-quality gown, Marianne studied herself in the mirror. *No more hiding out in my room*, she decided. Now that she had made her peace with Alexander, there was nobody else whose opinion she cared for - save Thomas and Ellen, of course, but she already knew she had their loyal support.

"I'm going down to join the rest of the company, Jean," she advised the maid, who was putting her letters in the pretty little writing-desk by one of the windows.

"Very good, my lady. I'll make sure Anne and Polly put all your things away just so." Jean puffed up a little with pride. "We'll spend the afternoon pressing wrinkles out of everything."

"You needn't do it all in one day," Marianne said, amused and touched by Jean's dedication. "Have the emerald silk ready for tonight and select another day dress for tomorrow, and the rest can wait."

"Never put off until tomorrow what you can do today, my ma always says," Jean answered with a smile. "You just leave it all to me, my lady."

Shaking her head, Marianne left Jean to her work and headed back downstairs. Arriving in the front hall as Ellen came out of the front parlour, she smiled at her friend. "I do apologise for abandoning you!"

"No apologies are needed; I heard your wardrobe had arrived! And indeed, I see it. What a beautiful dress!"

Preening a little, feeling happy to be wearing colours again, Marianne swished her skirts a little. "Isn't it pretty? Madame Fallou made it for me; do you know her shop?"

"I'm afraid not."

"I shall have to take you there when we get to London. She would love to dress you."

"Oh, but I have enough gowns already," Ellen disclaimed.

161

Laughing, Marianne linked her arm through her friend's. "Ellen, my dearest girl. You can *never* have too many gowns!"

Three more groups of guests arrived during the day, completing the roster of those who were to stay at Havers Hall for the house party. They crowded into the house, despite its large size, disturbing the equilibrium and Alexander's peace of mind. Unable to avoid company as he might have in his own home, he forced himself to be sociable with the other gentlemen Thomas had invited, and was agreeably surprised. To a man, they were sensible and intelligent, with conversation which did not bore him to tears. For the first time since leaving the army, Alex found himself among company which did not irritate him.

At least, when he was among the gentlemen. While the ladies were obviously intelligent too, almost all of them seemed to be inspecting him rather as though he were a horse they planned to put to stud; more than once he overheard comments about his fine legs and excellent teeth. Lady Alleyne was all but throwing Miss Alleyne at his head, and though Lady Serena Thorpe was too well-bred to make a spectacle of herself, she still made sure to put herself in situations where he was unable to avoid her entirely.

The one woman he would actually have liked to spend time with was no longer avoiding him, but she did not seem to have a particular desire for his company, either. Wearing the brightly coloured, beautifully tailored gowns from her newly delivered wardrobe, Marianne drew the eye everywhere she went.

Including his.

Especially his.

Alexander almost swallowed his tongue when she sailed into the drawing room that evening wearing the most beautiful green gown, her hair a mass of auburn curls atop her head. From the corner of his eye, he saw Viscount Thorpington drop his glass of sherry, gaping open-mouthed at the vision before him.

Mr. Alleyne was a little less gauche and quick to hurry to Marianne's side, but her glance at the younger man was nothing more than tolerant and amused, Alex saw now. His jealousy had blinded him before, but an evening spent watching Marianne gently fend off both Alleyne and Thorpington made it clear his accusation of her leading them on had been both unfounded and insulting. She gave neither of them the slightest encouragement; indeed, Alexander had cause to be grateful to her when she steered Thorpington in Miss Alleyne's direction, encouraging him to escort her into dinner.

Hoping to be seated beside Marianne at dinner, Alex was disappointed to find himself between Mrs. Pembroke and one of the new arrivals, a Miss Florence Wilson, who had arrived today with her twin sister Miss Fiona and their parents. A pleasant-looking girl if no great beauty, she was apparently too overwhelmed to speak at all, to him or even to kindly Sir Tobias Alleyne, seated on her other side.

Mrs. Pembroke was friendly enough, though she watched him with wary eyes, and his knowledge that she and Marianne were close kept him from paying too much attention to Marianne during the meal. He was still very aware of her at every moment. Seated on the other side of the table and two places down, it was easy enough for him to watch her surreptitiously, admire the way the candlelight gleamed on her fiery curls, drink in her low, musical laugh as she conversed comfortably with Mr. Wilson and Mr. Pembroke.

Even telling himself he was wasting his time, that Marianne had no interest in marrying again and he respected her too much to settle for anything less than marriage, he could not make himself look away. He should be trying to draw Miss Wilson out of her shell, discover what Ellen had seen in the girl, or maybe responding to Lady Serena's frequent smiles, or taking the many opportunities Lady Alleyne offered to get to know her daughter.

None of them appealed to him in the slightest. Marianne drew him to her like gravity: a force as inexorable as it was invisible.

"I believe you have an admirer in Lord Glenkellie," Mr. Pembroke murmured to Marianne as the dessert course was served. "But then, if I were not quite so in love with Amelia, I am sure I should join the ranks of your admirers as well," he added when she said nothing. "I do not doubt she has already pressed you to share the secret of your modiste."

Marianne smiled and chose to respond only to his latter remarks. "I hope Amelia will not put too much strain on your pocketbook."

"At least you've only your wife to spend on, Pembroke," Mr. Wilson grunted. "With twin daughters out at the same time, I swear my banker flinches every time I come to call! Ribbons and bonnets and new dancing slippers every week and I don't know what all."

"You will miss them when they are no longer in your house, I think," Marianne said wisely. Mr. Wilson was a crusty type with a heart of gold, she could already tell. His gaze softened whenever he looked on his wife or either of his daughters.

"Hm," Mr. Wilson muttered, but he nodded. "Have to be a special young man to win either of my girls. Shouldn't like them to be too far apart too. Very close, they are."

"They are quite identical. Tell me, do you insist they wear different colours so you can tell them apart?" Marianne teased gently.

"Oh, Mrs. Wilson and I always know. We make them do it to save other folks from embarrassment." Mr. Wilson give her a sly smile.

She laughed. Across the table, she caught Alexander's eye for the twentieth time and looked away hastily, a slight flush rising to her cheeks. Why *was* he looking at her so much? She had thought all was settled between them after their conversation that morning!

Though some of the men chose to linger in the dining room after dinner, the younger ones of the party chose to accompany the ladies back to the drawing room, where Mrs. Wilson pressed her daughters to perform for the company.

Alexander had chosen to accompany the ladies to Marianne's surprise; the previous evening he had lingered over port and cigars for quite some time. Tonight, he took a seat and accepted a cup of tea with every appearance of delight.

The Misses Wilson expressed reluctance, and Marianne sighed inwardly as their mother insisted. Why did some mothers press their daughters to exhibit in public constantly? She hoped the girls were not too uncomfortable. Finally they exchanged glances and moved to the pianoforte together, where they made a pretty picture in their pastel gowns, Florence in peach and Fiona in pale green.

Expecting an average performance, Marianne shot straight upright in her seat as Florence began to play. She was an exceptionally accomplished musician, true feeling showing through in her playing. Then Fiona began to sing, and all conversation in the room stopped as her voice soared.

Alexander appeared quite spellbound by the music, and Marianne found sudden envy welling in her breast. She had never shown any particular aptitude for music, plunking her way through required lessons in the pianoforte until her father decided to save the expense. It was the rare one of his economies she had not resented.

Now, watching Alexander's rapt face, she wished she had persevered. Perhaps if she had only practised harder - but no, her music teacher had only ever damned her with faint praise. Alexander would never have looked at her like that.

The enjoyment she had taken in the evening gone, Marianne sat back in her chair and sipped her tea. *It should not matter in the slightest if Alexander took pleasure in the playing and singing of two nice young ladies*, she tried to tell herself.

"You must get up next, Leonora!" a voice hissed behind her. Lady Alleyne, Marianne surmised. "'Tis obvious Lord Glenkellie has a fondness for music!"

"After this performance, I should sound like a cat caterwauling," Miss Alleyne replied softly.

Marianne hid her smile in her teacup. Miss Alleyne was no fool.

"I tell you, he is looking for a wife. If you do not put yourself in front of him, some other girl will be his marchioness!" Lady Alleyne snapped. Though she kept her voice low, Marianne's hearing was excellent and she heard every word quite clearly.

Miss Alleyne made no reply, and Marianne found herself examining Alexander's expression again as the Wilson sisters' spectacular performance drew to a close. He rose to applaud with the rest of the gentlemen, the reception a little more raucous than would be considered proper in London salons. But with an earl and a marquis leading the applause, who would reproach them?

Florence Wilson retreated back into her shell after the performance, taking a seat close to her mother, but Fiona preened as praise was heaped on her for her singing. Marianne added her compliments to the general praise, but a tiny ember of jealousy burned in her chest as Alexander kissed the girl's hand and declared she had the voice of an angel.

It is wrong for me to be envious, Marianne tried to tell herself firmly. She should be pleased Alexander planned to marry; he deserved happiness, after all. And he could do far worse than choosing one of the young ladies at Havers Hall; Ellen was an excellent judge of character.

So why did she feel absolutely miserable watching Miss Fiona Wilson smiling up at Alexander?

Chapter Fifteen

"A very pleasant way to spend an evening, wasn't it, Glenkellie?"

"Excuse me?" Jolted from his thoughts, Alexander turned to find Viscount Thorpington addressing him.

"Yesterday evening. I very much enjoyed it."

"So did I," Alex agreed. He'd been happily surprised, in truth; he couldn't recall the last time he'd enjoyed himself so much. The only small cloud had been Marianne's quiet mood; she had contributed little to the conversation after dinner and he had missed the bright wit and pertinent observations she always brought to any gathering. He could only assume it was his presence which had inhibited her; several times he had glanced up to find her eyes on him and her delicate brows creased in a frown.

"Miss Alleyne is rather lovely," Thorpington said, his tone almost questioning.

"A nice young lady," Alex agreed, his thoughts full of Marianne, but then he spotted the way the younger man's face fell. *Ah, so that was the way the wind blew.* "Very sweet," he added. "I understand her dowry is quite substantial, if you are considering her, Thorpington. Unexceptionable family, all things considered. Sir Tobias is very well thought of at the War Office, even if his wife is a little… well, I hesitate to say encroaching, but she is certainly ambitious."

Thorpington's smile was wry. "Lady Alleyne has nothing on my mother."

"Mine either." Alex smiled back, and companionable silence fell between them as they walked on. Thomas had organised a pheasant shoot for this morning, but Alex and Thorpington had so far not found a single bird, although they kept hearing shots in the distance. Perhaps the others were having better luck.

"So, uh," Thorpington said hesitantly after a while. "Leonora… Miss Alleyne, I mean…"

"The field is yours, Thorpington. Better jump in quick before the lady has her head turned by all the swains who will undoubtedly fall at her feet in London, though." Alexander gave him a nod, though the viscount certainly didn't need his permission.

"Thank you for your advice," Thorpington said with a grin. "But you're really not interested...?"

"As I said, she's a lovely girl. The important word being *girl*. No offence, but girls of Miss Alleyne's age seem very young to me."

"You're hardly in your dotage!"

Alex thumbed the scar on his cheek. "War ages a man," he said finally. "I spent too many years fighting, and sometimes it feels as though I aged five years for every one I was away from England. Miss Alleyne is scarcely out of the schoolroom - as is your sister, no offence intended."

"None taken. She has no ambitions in your direction, I assure you. Rather attached to an old school chum of mine, you see."

"Ah." Alex nodded sagely. "Thanks for the warning. Appreciate it. I'm sure I could fall violently in love with her if given the opportunity."

Thorpington laughed at his obviously disingenuous remark, then pointed. "Look there!"

They were both far too late raising their guns to get the bird, and Alex sighed as he lowered his.

"Pathetic. It's a good thing I'm not dependent on my marksmanship for my dinner any more."

"Any more?" Thorpington asked.

"Spain," Alex said, without offering any further explanation, and thankfully the younger man didn't press.

Giving up, they turned and walked back towards the Hall. The house was in sight when Thorpington spoke again. "Are the gossips wrong, then? You aren't looking for a wife?"

"No, I am," Alex admitted. "I wasn't expected to come into the title, but now that I have... well, the next heir after me isn't someone you'd want in charge of anything, much less a marquisate responsible for the livelihoods of thousands. He'd gamble the estate bankrupt within a month."

"So you need a wife to get an heir, but the debutantes are all too young for your tastes?" Thorpington summed up.

"Precisely."

"It's Lady Creighton, then?"

Alex tripped over his feet and almost measured his length on the grass, would have if not for Thorpington's hand under his elbow. "*What* did you say?" he stuttered, regaining his balance.

"Lady Creighton?" Thorpington's brow furrowed. "I mean… everyone's talking about the way you look at her. And her marriage was notoriously unhappy, but she's widowed now and perfectly respectable, unless you have doubts because she didn't give Creighton any children…"

"Oh dear God, please stop talking. And to think, I thought you were quiet!" Alex pressed a hand to his brow.

Thorpington flushed. "Only in the presence of ladies," he muttered. "They make me feel foolish."

"Ladies make fools of us all," Alex said dryly. "Especially if we are foolish enough to repeat gossip associated with them." He gave Thorpington a stern look. "Please don't mention Lady Creighton's name in any such gossip again."

"Yes, my lord." Thorpington had turned bright red with embarrassment. "I do beg your pardon, my lord."

Too much in turmoil to do more than nod acknowledgement, Alex strode back up the steps into the house, handing off his gun to Simons, who was waiting in the hall for him. "No luck today," he said shortly in response to the valet's querying expression.

"A shame, m'lord. If you would come into the boot room?"

He'd been about to storm off up the stairs but stopped in his tracks at the question. This wasn't his house, and it would be unpardonably rude to leave mud all over Havers Hall's pristine floors. Even if Thomas did employ an army of servants to keep them that way.

The other gentlemen had returned to the house - carrying quite a few birds between them, confound it - by the time Alex had his boots off. Unfortunately, he could not think of a graceful way to evade Thomas' invitation to join the others in the billiard room once he had cleaned up. Simons had wash water and a change of clothes ready in his room, and he was soon ready to proceed downstairs.

"Excuse me, Lord Glenkellie," Allsopp intercepted him in the front hall. "A letter just arrived for you." A silver tray was presented.

Alex frowned as he picked up the sealed letter. "Oh God, it's from my mother," he said in dismay, inspecting the impression in the wax seal.

"That bad?" Thomas asked, descending the stairs behind him.

Breaking the seal, Alex grimaced. "Probably."

"Step into my study to read it, if you like." Thomas gestured.

Alex accepted the invitation, sinking into a chair by the window to peer at his mother's script, so flamboyantly looped and embellished it was barely readable.

My Dear Alexander,

I am quite downcast not to find you in London.

"Christ, she's in London!"

Thomas, flicking through some papers on his desk, suppressed a snort at Alex's dismayed tone. Alex ignored him and kept reading.

I planned to spend some time with you before I depart for Italy in April. When you return to Town, we can begin your hunt for a bride. There seems quite a promising crop of debutantes this year; even though some of them are spending Christmas in the country, I have already seen a couple who would suit you. Do write to let me know when to expect you,

Your loving
Mother

"Damn!" Alex said, and then decided that was not nearly strong enough an exclamation. He let loose a stream of curses which made Thomas' eyes widen.

"Glenkellie! What in heaven's name has happened?"

"I'm going to have to go to London." Tossing the letter onto the fire in disgust, Alex shook his head. "My mother will have an announcement of my engagement in the newspapers by week's end otherwise."

"Engagement to *whom*?" Thomas asked in complete confusion.

"Whoever she decides will suit me best." Alex grimaced. "My mother is a force of nature, I'm afraid. Leaving her unsupervised in London is asking for trouble. She didn't have nearly such a wide circle of acquaintance at Glenkellie to aid and abet her mischief, you see, and she's quite capable of selecting a bride for me and telling me about it after she's already arranged things with the girl's family. I'm afraid I will have to go, if only to avoid being sued for breach of a promise she might make on my behalf."

"Of course, but we shall miss your company. Stay another night, at least; it's already noon, and by the time you're packed up it will be nearly dark. Leave at first light."

Thomas was right, of course. With a beleaguered sigh, Alex nodded his thanks. "I'm sorry to disrupt your plans - and I truly do regret having to leave your house party. I haven't enjoyed myself so much in a long time."

"That's good to hear, and we will miss your company. I'm glad you are staying tonight, at least; you can make your own apologies to Ellen. She would be most displeased if you skulked out without so much as a goodbye."

"I should not dare." Alex managed a smile. "I'll return to my rooms, if you don't mind, and start Simons on the packing. I'll rejoin you before dinner."

"Of course. Let Allsopp know if there's anything you need?"

"Thank you," Alex said.

Thomas nodded, heading towards the door before pausing as though struck by a sudden thought. "Actually - since you are headed for London, I wonder if I might ask your assistance with something?"

"Whatever I can do for you, you need only ask," Alex answered sincerely.

"Technically, it's not for me. Marianne - Lady Creighton - has some jewellery she wishes to sell, purchased for her by her late husband. I offered to assist her in the disposal of it for a fair price, but I wouldn't know where to start, apart from taking it back to the jewellers where it was purchased. Do you think you might be able to help?"

"My mother certainly would, even if I couldn't," Alex said wryly. "She has ever been fond of baubles."

Thomas laughed, taking a key from his pocket and unlocking a cupboard before removing a good-sized wooden box and placing it on the desk. "They all have provenance, which is how Marianne comes to be in possession of them. Creighton noted that they were hers specifically, rather than property of the Creighton estate. Even so, my agent had to practically wrest them from the new Earl. Tight-fisted type."

Glancing through the sheaf of receipts Thomas handed him, Alex nodded. "I see. And Mari - Lady Creighton doesn't want to keep any of them?"

"I suspect she can't stand the sight of them. Besides, she needs the funds; Creighton left her no dower income at all and the new Earl would apparently prefer to keep her beholden to him. Wants her as an unpaid companion to his wife and daughters."

Disgusted at hearing of this further insult to Marianne's dignity, Alex made a face. "Anything I can do to help, of course. Would you like me to only make enquiries, or to accept sales if I think I've achieved the best price for a piece?"

"Use your discretion. Marianne has barely a penny to her name and won't accept money from me or Ellen - yes, we've both tried. Do you know, her nieces pooled what they had and gave it to her so she could buy a ticket on the stage to get here? She *walked* the last part of the way." Thomas was clearly outraged on Marianne's behalf, and Alexander found his own fury rising again. "I will never understand why people don't treat family decently, especially when they have more than enough wealth to go around! My predecessor was just as bad; refused even to acknowledge Ellen as his distant cousin and turned her out with nowhere to go when her parents passed away!"

"Easy." Alex put a hand out to touch Thomas' arm lightly. "You and Ellen are doing God's work, believe in that. Marianne is lucky to have such supportive friends."

"I note you call her Marianne as well," Thomas said with a canny sideways glance. "Yet you have only known her a few days."

"I knew her much better many years ago. Wanted to marry her, in fact. Her father had other ideas."

"And now?"

"I beg your pardon?" Alex blinked.

181

"What's stopping you now? She's a respectable widow, and you're looking for a wife."

"She's not looking for a husband, that's what. Stop matchmaking, Thomas. You're dreadful at it."

Thomas laughed. "It was worth a try. I think the two of you would suit, as it happens. She's not intimidated by you, and you... well, you don't need a wealthy wife."

"I admit I have heard worse reasons for matching two people together. Undoubtedly, my mother's choices will be worse, much worse, so thank you for at least considering how the match might benefit both of us." Alex smiled, to show Thomas he was not offended. "Still, I think Marianne would value my friendship far more than the other, so please don't encourage any speculation." Picking up the wooden box and tucking the key Thomas offered into his waistcoat pocket, he vowed, "I will achieve the best prices I can for her jewels. A true friend would do no less."

Chapter Sixteen

London
Mid-January

"Aunt Marianne!"

Marianne barely held in her laughter as Diana and Clarissa made to throw themselves on her, before remembering at the last minute they were young ladies now and meant to act with decorum. They almost tripped over themselves, clutching at each other for support. The girls stumbled to a halt, straightened up, and made graceful curtseys, though the effect was rather ruined by what had preceded them.

Lavinia, seated by the fire in the drawing room of the Creighton townhouse, rolled her eyes to the heavens. "Girls!" she said in disgust.

"Restrain yourselves, please! This is not the country! What if Marianne's friend Lady Havers had accompanied her?"

"She did," Ellen said with a smile, stepping into the room behind Marianne. "Do forgive your butler for not introducing us, Lady Creighton. I'm afraid he was dealing with a matter related to one of your younger daughters. Something about a stray dog?"

Lavinia's mouth tightened, but she rose to her feet. "It is a pleasure to meet you at last, Lady Havers. May I present my daughters, Lady Diana and Lady Clarissa."

"I am delighted to meet you all," Ellen said with one of her disarmingly friendly smiles. "But please, do not let us be formal with each other; Marianne has told me so much about you I feel I know you all already. You must call me Ellen, and I shall call you Lavinia."

"I... well... of course." Lavinia looked rather as though she would prefer it otherwise, but the Havers earldom was a very old and wealthy one even if the current title holder was an American upstart and Ellen only the daughter of a country parson. Ellen Havers was also widely known to be on excellent terms with at least two of the patronesses of Almack's, which made her someone Lavinia dared not offend.

"Wonderful! Let us sit down and have a coze and get to know each other."

Marianne watched with amusement as Ellen took the seat immediately beside Lavinia. The formerly shy parson's daughter had become quite an impressive lady in the last year, confident in her position and her influence.

"Would you ring for tea, Clarissa?" Marianne requested, as Lavinia appeared slightly lost. Clarissa hurried to pull the bell, and then the two girls made a point of drawing Marianne to a sofa rather distant from where Ellen held their mother's attention captive.

"How long have you been in London?" Marianne asked. "We only arrived yesterday, and Ellen sent one of her footmen out directly to determine if the knocker was on your door; I was so pleased to hear it was."

"One week tomorrow," Diana reported. "And we have already visited a museum and a library and spent two whole days on Bond Street being fitted for new gowns."

Clarissa made a face at the latter. "I was never so bored in my life, nor stuck so many times with pins."

"Because you would not stop fidgeting," Diana smirked. Clarissa narrowed her eyes.

Marianne smiled, putting a hand on each girl's wrist to distract them. *They are still so very young*, she thought, and sisterly rivalry sparked between them often even though they were also best friends. They had no idea how lucky they were. What she would have given to have a sister she could confide in!

"So, we are here to ask if you would join our party at the theatre tomorrow night. Ellen insisted we must come in person to extend the invitation, and I was delighted to agree. I do hope your mother will accept."

Both girls immediately forgot their quibble and smiled with delight, falling over themselves to exclaim how gracious Lady Havers was to include them in her invitation.

"Do say we may go, Mama!" Clarissa cried out.

Lavinia pursed her lips. "You are not yet out, Clarissa," she said sternly.

"Why, this is the opera, not a ball," Ellen said serenely. "It is quite unexceptionable for a girl Clarissa's age not yet out to attend *some* social events, you know. I consider it excellent practice for her own Season. Private dinner parties, public events such as the opera or exhibitions, even picnics when the weather improves. Of course, she cannot be courted yet, but I think it very unfair for younger sisters to be entirely excluded from the fun. How old are your younger children, again?"

"Our son Charles is fifteen, Lucinda fourteen and Penelope twelve," Lavinia said a little ungraciously. "I hope you do not suggest we take *them* to the opera!"

"Of course not!" Ellen looked shocked. "Evening events are quite out of the question. Nevertheless, I intend to host a picnic and a few luncheons later in the year, and I do hope you will bring them along."

"I was included in many events from the age of ten or so, when we lived in London," Marianne put in. "With my governess in attendance, of course. Have you found someone suitable yet, Lavinia?" It could not hurt to press the point that she would not be available at Lavinia's convenience. She would not put it past Lavinia to try and fob the younger girls off on her at events, and while she did not mind chaperoning Clarissa and Diana on occasion, she had no intention of sitting at the children's table.

"Arthur and I interviewed candidates this week," Lavinia said sulkily. "We offered a suitable candidate the post, and she begins on Monday."

"Excellent," Marianne said with a nod, holding Lavinia's eyes until the other woman flushed and looked away.

"You intend to remain with the Havers then, Aunt Marianne?" Clarissa murmured as Ellen asked Lavinia another question, ending the awkward silence.

"For the time being, at least. Though I miss you girls, I'm afraid living in your parents' household was not a comfortable situation for me."

Diana squeezed her hand sympathetically. "We quite understand," she said, her voice soft. "Mama and Papa have changed since Papa inherited the earldom. We are no longer permitted to associate with our friends, girls we went to school with, because they are not situated high enough in life. Everyone else is now lesser, just because of an accident of birth."

Marianne shook her head with an impatient sigh. "Foolish," she muttered. "If your mother treats anyone without a title as lesser, she will quickly make enemies of some of the most powerful people in London."

"She's determined Diana must marry an earl at least," Clarissa said. "She has been making lists of all the unmarried peers in London."

"Some of them are older than Papa!" Diana's look of horror was unfeigned.

Marianne clasped her niece's hand, shaken to the core at the thought of history repeating. "I won't let you be forced into marriage to any man not of your choosing. Either of you," she declared passionately. "I swear it."

"How wonderful this is!" Diana whispered, clutching at Marianne's arm as they took their seats in the front row of the Havers box. Lavinia sat on Diana's other side, trying to hide her own wonder as she gazed around the brightly lit theatre and the glittering throng taking their seats. Clarissa sat at the end, hands folded demurely in her lap, but her eyes were bright with interest as she took in everything around her.

Ellen had insisted Marianne and her nieces take the front row, while she sat behind with Thomas and Arthur. Only Marianne realised it was no sacrifice for Ellen to sit beside Thomas and hold his hand throughout the performance, rather than sit in the front row under full scrutiny of the interested audience.

Marianne had already seen any number of friends, a lot of them waving and smiling. Rather too many men - she hesitated to call them gentlemen - of her acquaintance were eyeing her blue dress with a blue and silver cape, smiling invitingly at her. Sighing, she mentally girded herself for the propositions she would no doubt have to waste far too much of her time rejecting, gently and otherwise. At least staying with the Havers would give her protection from the most importunate, who might be inclined to persist if she had her own household.

"Do you know that gentleman, Aunt Marianne?" Diana asked then.

"Don't point, dear." Marianne caught Diana's hand on the way up, pressing it back to her lap. "Just direct with your eyes, and describe him."

"The box across the way," Diana said, blushing at having almost made a gauche mistake. "The tall, handsome gentleman with a scar, in a blue coat in a box directly across the theatre. There is an older lady with him wearing a burgundy dress; she has a lot of feathers in her hair."

"Oh!" Marianne smiled as she saw Alexander, standing in his box looking directly at her. "That is Alexander Rotherhithe, Marquis of Glenkellie, and though I am not acquainted with her that must be his mother with him, the Dowager Marchioness."

"A *marquis*?" Diana looked as though she might faint.

Lavinia immediately leaned across her. "And is there a current Marchioness of Glenkellie, Aunt?"

"No," Marianne said, and honesty compelled her to admit, "I believe he is in the market for a wife, however. He is but lately come to the title; he spent quite a few years in the army and on the Continent."

"A war hero, too?" Lavinia looked delighted. "You must introduce us at the interval, Aunt!"

Marianne was saved from having to answer by Ellen leaning forward and saying "I must stake a prior claim, Lavinia; I want to introduce you to Sarah Child Villiers, Lady Jersey. I spy her here tonight and we must appeal to her for vouchers to Almack's."

"Oh, yes, that is infinitely more important," Marianne said, relieved Ellen had stepped in to distract Lavinia's attention. "You can meet Glenkellie another time, but you will have only one opportunity to make a good first impression on Lady Jersey."

Thankfully, that made Lavinia subside into nervous silence as the curtain opened and the performance began.

At the interval, Ellen lost no time in hurrying Lavinia off to meet Lady Jersey, asking Thomas and Arthur to get some refreshments and Marianne to remain in the box with Diana and Clarissa -- a request Marianne was more than happy to honour.

Beckoning Clarissa to move one seat closer so they could hear each other over the din of the audience, Marianne asked the girls how they were enjoying the play and listened indulgently to their excited chatter.

When the door opened behind her, she glanced around, assuming Thomas and Arthur were returning. The tall figure entering the box, however, accompanied by the lady in the burgundy dress with the mass of feathers in her hair, was Alexander.

Chapter Seventeen

Spotting Marianne at the theatre was a stroke of luck. Thomas had sent around a note letting Alex know the Havers party had arrived in London, but he had been fully tied up with business and engagements with his mother -- who was utterly determined to see him married before she departed for Italy in April. He hardly dared let her out alone in case she promised him to some bacon-brained chit.

Marianne's jewellery had been remarkably easy to dispose of. Garrard's had been delighted to assist, telling him the former Earl of Creighton had always wanted their most unusual and collectible pieces for his wife, many of which had now increased in value. They suggested an agent who quickly found buyers for almost all the pieces, in some cases achieving a price a good deal in excess of the original purchase price. Alex had engaged Mr. Coutts to open a bank account in Marianne's name, depositing all the monies into it, and was eager to give her the good news.

Therefore, at the interval, he insisted his mother accompany him to the Havers box. Intrigued by the possibility of meeting the American arl she'd heard was busy setting Parliament on its ear with his radical ideas, she agreed.

Despite seeing Thomas in the passageway, Alex nodded and walked straight on past him. It had just occurred to him that his mother, impossible though she could be, might actually be his best ally in convincing Marianne marriage might suit her. Most especially if Alexander were the groom. If the last two weeks of being paraded before every marriageable young woman in London had done anything, it had convinced him Marianne was still the only woman who could possibly make him happy. Whether he could make her so remained to be seen, but he was willing to spend the rest of his life trying.

Marianne's startled expression as she rose to her feet and dipped a curtsey immediately had Alex second-guessing whether he should have waited to introduce his mother to her. "Lady Creighton." He bowed formally. "Mother, please allow me to present Marianne, Lady Creighton to you? Lady Creighton, my mother Lady Helena, the Dowager Marchioness of Glenkellie."

"Lady Glenkellie." Marianne gave a lower, more respectful curtsey.

"Are you the widow or the new one?" Lady Helena Glenkellie asked bluntly.

Marianne's lips twitched slightly, and Alex knew she'd bitten back a laugh. "I'm the widow, my lady. My niece the Countess has just stepped out with Lady Havers to go and meet Lady Jersey, I believe."

"Ah, Sarah." Alex's mother smirked. "Need vouchers, do you? For these two gels, or yourself?"

"Lady Jersey is a friend of mine already, my lady. Pray, allow me to make known to you Lady Diana Creighton and Lady Clarissa Creighton," Marianne said, and the two girls sank into deep curtseys, expressions of awe on their faces. "I call them my nieces; it is easier than explaining the complexities of our actual relationship. Diana, Clarissa; Lord Glenkellie and Lady Helena Glenkellie."

"Both out, are you?" Alex's mother examined the two girls with a critical eye. Alex could have told her the answer from their dress; while Diana was wearing a lovely white gown with a faint silver stripe in it, perfect for a debutante, Clarissa's dark blue gown with tiny white spots was much more plain and demure.

"Lady Diana is making her come-out this Season," Marianne replied. "Clarissa is only just seventeen and will wait until next year, though her parents are permitting her to attend some social events to gain experience."

"Very wise, too." Lady Glenkellie cast one more glance over Clarissa before obviously dismissing her and turning her full attention to Diana. She seemed to like what she saw, because she glanced at Alex and smiled. "Do you attend the Balford ball on Friday, Lady Diana?"

"I don't believe we have been invited, my lady," Diana said in a small voice, looking nervously at Marianne.

"I shall ensure you receive an invitation. The Duchess of Balford is a particular friend of mine." Lady Glenkellie nodded imperiously.

"That is most generous of you, my lady." Marianne curtseyed again, and Diana and Clarissa followed her lead.

The dowager marchioness looked back at Marianne and blinked, almost as though she had forgotten her presence. "Yes. Well. I daresay we shall see you there, shan't we, Alexander?"

"I look forward to it greatly," Alex said, with a smile at Marianne.

"You should ask Lady Diana for a dance now. No doubt she will be swarmed with eager young swains before you get a look in, otherwise."

Alex gaped at his mother in surprise. *She's got entirely the wrong end of the stick*, he thought. "Ah… yes," he said, caught out by the unexpected manoeuvre. "Lady Diana, might I request a dance with you at the Balford ball?"

"The *first* dance," his mother pushed.

Diana looked at Marianne, wide-eyed. Marianne nodded encouragingly.

"I should be honoured, Lord Glenkellie," the girl said shyly, blushing scarlet.

"Excellent. I take it we will not have the pleasure of your company, Lady Clarissa?"

"I regret you are correct." Clarissa smiled at him, apparently a little less shy than her older sister. "Balls are quite out of the question for me this year, I'm afraid."

"It is Society's loss." Alexander bowed his head to her. "In that case, Lady Marianne, might I solicit the honour of your hand for the *second* dance?"

Marianne looked utterly startled. Diana and Clarissa looked quite delighted, and his mother - his mother turned to him with her mouth wide open with shock.

"Alexander, what are you *doing*?" she demanded.

"I am asking a delightful lady, whom I consider to be a good friend, to reserve me a dance at a ball we will both attend," Alex said, trying to sound calm and placid, as though dancing with Marianne wasn't one of the most desirable things he could imagine.

"Well," Marianne said uncertainly. "I had not intended to dance…"

"But Aunt Marianne, you keep telling us how much you miss dancing!" Clarissa said, and Alex shot her a grateful glance. The minx gave him a conspiratorial wink, and he bit back a shout of laughter. She, at least, knew precisely what he was about.

"I do miss dancing." Marianne nibbled on her lower lip briefly before giving a decisive nod. "I am my own woman these days, beholden to nobody else's good opinion of me. Very well, Lord Glenkellie, I should be delighted to give you the second dance at the Balford ball."

Alex couldn't restrain his smile of triumph. With a kiss to Marianne's hand, he followed his mother from the Havers box and back around to the other side of the theatre, knowing once they were away from prying ears, the interrogation would come. The Dowager Marchioness of Glenkellie missed nothing.

"What are you thinking!" his mother hissed as soon as they were once again seated in their own box. "Wasting your time asking that woman for a dance!"

"Why is it a waste of my time?" He raised his eyebrows at her.

"Because you need someone to give you an heir, and in eight years of marriage, she didn't conceive once." Lady Helena pursed her lips and shook her head.

"Mother, Creighton had three wives and *none* of them ever conceived. Does that not suggest perhaps the fault might not be with the wives?" Alexander had taken the time to research the late earl once he arrived back in London, and been horrified by what he found. Both Countesses of Creighton prior to Marianne had not lived into their thirties, their deaths unexplained.

The suggestion gave his mother pause. "Best not to risk it, nevertheless," she said. "You should choose a girl from a family of proven breeders. One of those younger Creighton girls will do nicely, if you want to ally yourself with the family; there's a whole pack of them, I believe, though they're mostly girls."

"They're *children*, Mother."

"You're barely ten years Lady Diana's senior!" Still, she frowned when he just looked back at her. "You are quite set on her, then?"

"If she will have me."

"She's a fool if she won't." The dowager marchioness snorted magnificently, looking back across the theatre to where Marianne sat talking with her nieces, now rejoined by Thomas and Arthur. "She's very beautiful, I suppose," she said, "but how well do you really know her?"

Alex smiled. "Do you remember my letters home, from Portugal and Spain?"

"Indeed I do, infrequent though they were." His mother tapped him on the knee with her fan. "I was constantly trying to convince you to leave the army and come home where it was safe, but your letters were full of how you were making a difference out there."

"And?" he pressed. "Do you recall anything else I said?"

"Oh, there was some nonsense about how you couldn't bear to come back to England because the girl you were in love with had thrown you over and married some wealthy old earl..." the marchioness tapered off, her eyes widening. "*No*. You don't mean *her*?"

"The Honourable Miss Marianne Abingdon," Alex said wistfully. "We were both young and naive, and while she promised to wait for me, her father's gambling debts were such that a valuable asset like a daughter hailed as the most beautiful girl in London wasn't to be wasted on the likes of me, fourth in line with naught but an army commission to my name."

"Oh Alex." Lady Helena's eyes were soft as she laid her hand over his. "She didn't throw you over, did she?"

"No, but until recently I thought she had. Instead it transpires she was basically sold to a man three times her age and spent years in a desperately unhappy, even abusive, marriage."

"The poor girl, how perfectly dreadful!" His mother sounded quite outraged on Marianne's behalf. "I was one of the great beauties in my day, too, and my father was outraged I 'threw myself away' on a younger son, but he would never have forced me to marry someone I did not want!"

Lady Helena was the daughter of a duke, and her dowry had been more than substantial. Even though his father was the younger son, Alexander had always known there would be a substantial inheritance in his future. He'd also always known his parents loved each other. Indeed, he suspected his mother had become more difficult since his father's death mainly because she missed her husband so. Lord Patrick Rotherhithe had always indulged his wife's slightest whim.

"I love her," Alex admitted, knowing his mother was now firmly on his side. "I've always loved her, and I want no one else for my wife. Unfortunately, after her terrible marriage, she has decided she prefers not to remarry."

"Then we will simply have to convince her otherwise, won't we, darling?" Lady Helena patted his hand and smiled. "You just leave it to me."

"I'd really rather not." He winced, thinking of the chaos his mother might engender with her machinations.

She laughed, unfazed by his lack of confidence in her. "Young men do like to do their own wooing, I suppose. Well, I will spend my time filling her ears with tales of how wonderful my marriage was, and how like your father you are."

"That would be very helpful, Mother," Alex said sincerely.

"You are, you know." His mother reached up and touched his cheek gently. "Very much like him. He'd be very proud - and so would your grandfather, if he'd truly had the chance to know you. Don't hold Duncan's dying words against him. He was grieving for both his sons, you must remember. He pored over every newspaper account of the battles you fought in, and every time you were mentioned in dispatches or bestowed with a medal, he would give a toast in your honour at dinner."

"He did?" Startled, Alex blinked. "I didn't know that."

"You never had much chance to know him, being away at school, then university, then the army. I wish you'd known him better." His mother looked back across the theatre at Marianne. "I think he'd have liked her, you know. He'd have said something about her looking like a proper Scot, with that red hair."

Alex took his mother's hand. "Let's see about persuading her to marry into a good Scots family then, shall we?"

Chapter Eighteen

Marianne found herself utterly unable to concentrate on the rest of the play. She was far too aware of Alexander and his mother only a short distance away, heads bent towards each other in intense conversation, both of them with eyes fixed firmly on the box where she sat the whole time. The dowager marchioness had clearly been quite keen on Alexander getting to know Diana, and it would certainly be a good match for her niece.

Not only that, but Marianne knew firsthand exactly how decent a man Alexander was. He would surely take good care of Diana, make sure she wanted for nothing. Diana, with her sweet nature, could not help but love him, and would surely be loved in return.

So why did the very idea make Marianne feel sick to her stomach?

She could not stop Diana and Clarissa excitedly telling their mother about meeting a marquis and his mother, and being invited to a duchess' ball, of course. Or Clarissa needling her sister about being asked for the first dance.

Lavinia could hardly contain her excitement, and Marianne was praised to the skies for being the means of introduction to such exalted personages. "Dancing with a marquis at a duchess' ball!" she kept saying, as though she could not quite believe it. "My little girl!"

"Lord Glenkellie asked Aunt Marianne for the second," Diana said innocently.

"Oh, that was just politeness," Marianne said quickly as Lavinia's brows drew down in a frown. "We are old friends, after all. He could hardly *not* ask. And you were quite right, I do miss dancing. Not many gentlemen will request a set with an old widow like me, so I shall enjoy the opportunities when they come my way." Her tone was a little defiant as she met Lavinia's gaze, and the older woman nodded after a moment, shrugging.

"So long as you do not distract Diana's prospects, all will be well." It was Arthur who whispered malevolently into her ear.

Marianne's jaw clenched, but she pretended he had not spoken and stared fixedly at the stage, though in truth she took in little of the rest of the play.

The following morning as Ellen and Marianne took breakfast together, Ellen confided Lady Jersey had not been prepared to offer vouchers without meeting Diana. Thus, Ellen had promised to collect Lavinia and Diana in her carriage and take them to call on Lady Jersey for tea that afternoon.

"Lady Jersey insisted I bring you along as well, of course," she said.

"I should rather keep Clarissa company," Marianne said quickly. "Perhaps we might take a walk in the park."

"Are you avoiding Lady Jersey?" Ellen's gaze was uncomfortably sharp. "It's quite all right if you are, of course. I'll happily assist - though I should like to know why."

With a sense of relief that she need not mislead Ellen, Marianne said, "I think she will try and persuade me to marry again. She fancies herself a matchmaker; only look how many young men she tried to throw in your way, and she barely had any opportunities before Thomas snatched you up!"

"True," Ellen admitted. She gave Marianne another penetrating look. "And you are quite sure you will never marry again?"

"I could never wish to be under any man's control again," Marianne said frankly. "I will fight Arthur to retain what independence I have, and God willing, with good friends like you and Thomas and the Pembrokes, I shall contrive to live well enough to suit me."

"You will have a place with us always, if you wish it," Ellen promised. "As a valued member of the family, not merely a guest."

Tears of emotion choked Marianne's throat, and she reached out to touch Ellen's hand, her expression full of gratitude.

The clatter of hooves and wheels just outside broke the moment, and they both looked to the window to see a carriage drawn up at the front door.

"That's the Glenkellie crest on the door," Ellen noted. "I think perhaps you have a visitor, Marianne."

"It's rather too early for morning calls." Marianne shook her head, regaining her composure. "I am sure he is only here because he has some business with Thomas."

Footsteps in the hallway and the sound of the study door opening and closing seemed to confirm her supposition, and the two ladies returned to their toast and tea.

Only a few moments later, though, Thomas entered the room. "I do beg your pardon," he said, "but Glenkellie is here to discuss some matters of business with Marianne."

"With me?" Marianne looked blank. "What business could he have to discuss with me?"

But Ellen was already getting up and saying she had a hundred jobs to do and she would leave them to it.

Marianne had little choice but to set her teacup aside and follow Thomas to his study, a smaller room than the one at Havers Hall but no less comfortably furnished.

Alex was waiting there, smiling as he saw her enter the room. "Lady Marianne." He bowed as Thomas escorted her to a seat and then both men took their seats as well.

"Whatever is this about?" she asked in confusion.

"Do you recall I advised you that I had commissioned Glenkellie to see what might be done about your jewellery?" Thomas asked.

"Oh." She had tried to forget everything about the hated jewels. "Yes, I suppose so. Are they worth anything?" she asked, turning to face Alexander.

"A good deal, as it turns out. Some four thousand pounds, all told. I've placed the money in an account at Coutts Bank in your name. If you would at some time make an appointment to accompany me there, I can vouch to Mr. Coutts that the money is yours and then you will be able to do with it whatever you wish."

"Four *thousand* pounds?" Marianne said, flabbergasted.

"Indeed, and there are still some small pieces remaining, plus a necklace my mother wishes to purchase as a gift for her sister, who she intends to visit in Italy this year."

Completely stunned, Marianne merely sat and blinked at him, at least until Thomas said, "Marianne, are you feeling quite well? You've turned pale."

"I just," she turned to him and shook her head. "Four thousand pounds - I never expected so much!"

"You are quite an heiress," Thomas said, teasing. "All the fortune hunters will be chasing after you when they learn of it. For it is yours alone, not a widow's portion you would lose should you remarry."

"But what am I to do with so much money?" For all Creighton's wealth, Marianne had never carried more than a few shillings in her own purse. Everything she purchased was sent on account to her husband.

"We both stand ready to advise you, should you wish," Alex said, and she looked back at him. "Or Mr. Coutts could make some recommendations, if you would like to consult with an independent party. Even placed in the four per cents, though, you would get an income of some one hundred and sixty pounds per annum, which would be more than sufficient to rent a house and keep some servants, if you wish."

"Or you can continue to reside with us, and save the money for the future," Thomas said with a frown at Alexander. "I know Ellen wishes you to remain with us, as one of the family, and your being a woman of means does not change that."

"I will have to think about it," Marianne said at last.

"Whatever you decide to do, I stand ready to assist," Alexander said. "In fact, if it is convenient, I am available to convey you to the bank this morning."

"I think that's a good idea," Thomas encouraged, and Marianne was persuaded to go and collect a coat and hat and ask Jean to accompany her.

"To avoid any appearance of impropriety," she told her maid, "though of course there wouldn't be any; Lord Glenkellie is a perfect gentleman."

"Still, you don't want folks gossiping about you bein' alone with a man," Jean said wisely, putting on her own coat. "I don't mind goin' for a ride in a fancy carriage at all, m'lady. Never been out of Herefordshire before, have I? London's full of wonders to see."

With Jean sitting beside her absorbed in the sights passing by outside the carriage window, Marianne found her eyes resting on Alexander. He looked the picture of a fine London gentleman, though he eschewed the bright colours worn by the foppish, his clothes were perfectly tailored to fit him, and she did not doubt the shine on his boots alone was hard-earned by dedicated hours of polishing by some under-servant.

"Thank you for assisting me in this matter, Lord Glenkellie," she said impulsively.

"You're most welcome." Alexander smiled at her. "I admit I was surprised to find the jewels of such value, but pleased on your behalf." He paused a moment before adding, "You paid a high price for them."

She had not considered it that way, but now that she did, she smiled wryly. "Indeed, I was quite expensive, was I not? Five hundred a year... he could have kept several mistresses for that, if he had wished."

Alexander looked horrified at her flippant remark. "Dear God, never say so!" he exclaimed. "Crei - *that man* valued you far too cheaply!"

Appreciative he had recalled she did not like to hear the name Creighton, and touched by his outrage on her behalf, Marianne gave him a rueful shrug. "I admit I do not know what he paid my father. Several thousand at least, I must suppose. I understand his gambling debts were quite substantial."

"A good woman is a pearl beyond price," Alexander said, and then he leaned forward, gazing at her intently. "The *love* of a good woman cannot be purchased, not for money or jewels or any such thing."

Jean let out a tiny sigh beside her, and Marianne had to admit it was a deeply romantic sentiment. Alexander's intense blue gaze was making her feel a little uncomfortable, though, so she only murmured, "Indeed, you are correct," before turning her head and looking out at the streets.

Mr. Coutts was a rather elderly gentleman, Marianne discovered, in his late seventies, but as professional and charming as Marianne could wish. He listened while Alexander verified her identity and then turned his full attention to Marianne.

"My bank is at your disposal, Lady Creighton. Your funds are at the present time lodged in an account which attracts only minimal interest; I would not recommend keeping more than the amount you would require in, say, a twelve-month period there at any one time."

"I am not presently decided on what, if any, investments I wish to make," Marianne admitted.

"When you are, my lady, we stand ready to assist. Do you wish to withdraw any funds for your own use at this time?"

"It's up to you," Alexander said when she hesitated. "You might wish to have some small amount on hand for expenses - a few pounds, perhaps? Remember, there is more to come when the rest of the sales are concluded, and you can return on any day the bank is open to make a further withdrawal if you wish."

"Ten pounds," Marianne decided. "That is a sufficient sum for any small purchases, I believe. If

I wish to make a larger purchase than that, it would be as well to meditate on it a day or two anyway."

"A very prudent attitude, my lady," Mr. Coutts approved. "Small notes would be best, I think? A few moments, and I will have one of my tellers complete the transaction."

Within minutes, Marianne was tucking a small roll of pound and ten-shilling notes into her reticule, along with a small pouch containing a pound in coins. Taking their leave of Mr. Coutts, they collected Jean from the anteroom where the maid waited and returned to the carriage.

"Would you like to return directly to Cavendish Square, or may I convey you elsewhere?" Alexander enquired.

It took Marianne a few moments to reply. She was still too accustomed to having her every move dictated by others, she realised; the need to ask permission to go anywhere or do anything had become ingrained.

"I would like to go somewhere, yes," she said finally. "Would you perhaps have time to take a walk with me?"

"I should be delighted," Alexander replied promptly. "Though it is cold today, it is quite dry. St. James's Park isn't far from here, just along The Strand?"

He was asking, not telling, her where they should go, his hand extended to help her up into the carriage and his driver awaited her instruction.

A heady feeling enveloped Marianne, a rush of lightness, almost as though she was floating. "I should love to go to St. James's Park. Could we perhaps make a stop by a baker's shop to buy some bread? I have ever been fond of feeding the ducks there."

"You heard Lady Marianne," Alexander said to his driver as he handed Jean up after her mistress, "a baker's shop and then the park. Hungry ducks await!"

Chapter Nineteen

Arriving back at the Havers' townhouse with muddy shoes and cheeks pink from the cold Marianne could not wipe the broad smile from her face as she accompanied Jean upstairs to change.

"You look pleased with yourself," Ellen said as they met on the landing. "Did you enjoy your outing?"

"I fed the ducks!" Marianne said, laughing as she realised she sounded like an excited child.

Ellen's expression was both puzzled and amused as she tilted her head slightly and said, "That does sound like fun. Are you coming with me this afternoon?"

"Oh, why not. Lady Jersey will only turn up here to see me if I do not, and probably bring a selection of potential suitors with her. At least if I go, I can impress on her the need to see Diana well-settled." Still in a good mood, Marianne shrugged off her earlier concerns. "When do you wish to go?"

"Will a half hour be enough time to refresh yourself?"

"Easily!"

Ellen smiled, obviously delighted by Marianne's happy mood. "I'll have Cook send up a little luncheon for you - some soup perhaps?"

"Begging your pardon, m'lady, but I sent the instruction to the kitchen already." Jean bobbed a curtsey.

"Good girl, Jean. I'm glad Marianne has someone so devoted to her comfort." Ellen praised and Jean blushed, ducking her head shyly.

"Jean is wonderful, and I fully intend to steal her from your employ," Marianne said. "Now I have control of some funds of my own, I hope she will accept the position of my personal maid on a permanent basis."

Jean's eyes shone with unshed tears as she curtseyed again, deeper this time. "Oh, m'lady. I'm that honoured. But don't you want one of them proper French lady's maids?"

"A fine English girl is more than good enough for me," Marianne told her.

"Then you should accept Lady Marianne's offer, with my blessing," Ellen declared.

Jean wasn't the type to repeatedly babble thanks, for which Marianne was quite grateful as they proceeded to her rooms. The fire was soon built up, Marianne's muddy boots and damp gown removed, fresh things laid out for her to change into, and a tray arrived from the kitchen with a light snack to sate her hunger.

"I used to take such service for granted, perhaps because of how grudgingly it was offered," Marianne murmured as Jean took a brush and began attending to her hair, "yet now, I am almost overwhelmed with gratitude for Lady Havers' kindness and your good care of me, Jean."

"Lady Havers has naught but good to say about you, m'lady," Jean said, tucking in a stray curl, "and as for me - well, it's a pleasure to look after you and all your lovely things. You've only kind words for everyone. Believe me, servants notice who ain't so sweet-tempered."

"I'm sure you do." Marianne hesitated, then thought she might as well ask. "Did any of the servants at Havers Hall speak much of Lord Glenkellie? I know he was only there a few days, before he had to return to London, and he brought his own manservant with him, so perhaps they didn't have much to do with him."

"Not so much, you're right, my lady, but everyone as did serve him said he was right civil, 'specially for bein' so high a lord, you know. And his man Simons was fair devoted. Said as how Lord Glenkellie is the best master he could ask for, and everyone who serves him thinks the same. Me, I think anyone Lord and Lady Havers choose as a friend must be one of the finest people in England," Jean insisted. "They chose you, didn't they?"

Marianne chuckled. "Well, one could say I rather thrust myself upon them, in fact, but I will accept your compliment at face value, Jean. For I too think Lord and Lady Havers are excellent judges of character."

Lady Jersey received their little group in her fabulously overdecorated Indian parlour. Marianne, who had been there once before, stifled laughter as Ellen and the Creighton ladies looked around agape. Catching Sarah Child Villiers' eye, she had to look away to compose herself.

Ellen finally pulled herself together to present Lavinia, Diana, and Clarissa to Lady Jersey. Though Clarissa had not technically been invited, Lavinia had insisted she come along anyway, and received exactly what she deserved for her presumption. Lady Jersey looked Clarissa up and down once and said, "Should you not be in the schoolroom, child? There are some kittens in the mews, I believe; go with Frost to see them and Cook shall give you a glass of milk after."

Clarissa was quite obviously laughing as she left in the wake of the imperious butler, and Diana's longing expression said she would far rather be going with her sister than sitting down to take tea with one former and three current countesses.

Marianne didn't blame Diana. She would rather be going to the stables too than face another Lady Jersey interrogation, but the arbiter of the Ton was a very perceptive woman who had seen past the aloof face Marianne had been forced to present to the world by her husband, had been kind to her and invited her into her circle of friends. It was a debt of kindness Marianne could never repay, so she settled herself on a chaise, pasted on an attentive expression, and accepted a lemon biscuit.

"So you're Diana." Sarah inspected the quaking debutante with a gimlet eye. "What's your dowry again, girl?"

"Ten thousand pounds," Lavinia said smugly, "and Clarissa will have as much next year."

Lady Jersey turned her gaze on Lavinia. Not a word was said, but Lavinia shrank back into her seat and clamped her lips shut.

"What do you like, Diana?" Lady Jersey asked, and Diana gulped, glancing at her mother. Lavinia nodded.

"I am accomplished on the pianoforte and sing tolerably well," Diana said in a small voice. "I enjoy needlework and drawing with pencils. I speak French and some Italian…"

"Same as every other young woman of your rank this season, if not a little less," Lady Jersey said with a sniff, and Diana looked as though she might cry. Sarah's tone softened. "I mean, what do you *like*? What do you enjoy doing, if you have nobody to please but yourself?"

"Oh," Diana said, obviously surprised. "Well… I really do like drawing. Animals in particular. I drew Father's dogs, Apollo and Ares, and Father liked it so much he had it framed and hung it on the wall of his study."

Lady Jersey nodded encouragingly. "Animals are good. Many young men are very fond of their dogs and horses. If you are able, for example, to draw each of his horses well enough to show its distinguishing features, he will very likely declare himself in love with you on the instant."

222

Diana let out a laugh before recalling herself and turning it into a ladylike giggle behind her hand. Sarah winked at Marianne, and she let out a sigh of relief. Diana had managed to endear herself to Sarah, and the influential countess would throw her in the path of not only eligible young men, but ones whom she might like and respect.

"Well, I think you'll take very well, my dear," Lady Jersey said, giving her stamp of approval. "I hope you'll take my advice, which is to always let young men know what you're really thinking. Girls who pretend they're hanging on an idiot's every word tend to find themselves married to the idiot in question."

Ellen laughed at that; Lavinia was staring pop-eyed and indignant, but still too intimidated to speak.

"I must agree," Marianne said, drawing Diana's eyes to her. "A man who will not respect your opinions and your wishes is not a man you would want to become more closely acquainted with. Do not wait until you are already committed to let him know who you truly are."

"I will endeavour always to keep that in mind," Diana said. "Thank you for your advice, Lady Jersey. Aunt Marianne."

"Speaking of advice," Lady Jersey said, "I understand you have spent very little time in London, Lady Creighton?"

Lavinia flushed and looked a little angry to be called on so, but she answered. "Yes, my lady, that's so. My parents did not care to travel much from Durham, where our home was, and where I met my husband."

"You should listen carefully to your aunt." Sarah indicated Marianne. "She has successfully navigated the dangerous waters of London's upper society for years now. Allow her to guide your daughters and they will do very well."

Lavinia spluttered. "But - but - Marianne isn't married!"

"You make an excellent point." There was a familiar, wicked glint in Sarah's eye. "Do you have any suitable candidates in mind, Marianne?"

"I think your ladyship knows perfectly well that I do not wish to remarry." Marianne remained cool and composed, her hands folded in her lap.

"You cannot let one bad experience put you off for life. 'Tis rather like riding a horse; you fall off, you must get right back on!"

"Nevertheless," Marianne said levelly.

"Well, we shall see. I shan't press you, not this year, but I think 'twould be a shame if you closed yourself off from the possibility entirely." Sarah's voice was quite gentle. "You have a great capacity to love, my dear. I would not like to see you wasted as a lonely widow forever."

Marianne looked down, tears pricking at the back of her eyelids. "Thank you for your concern, my lady, but I pray you do not trouble yourself over me. I am very content as I am and wish only to focus on seeing my dear nieces well-settled."

There was a long moment of silence, and Marianne finally lifted her eyes to glance at Sarah, finding the other woman studying her with a slight frown. Essaying a small smile, Marianne prayed her friend would accept her decision.

"Very well," Lady Jersey said finally. "Lady Creighton, I am pleased to advise your application for subscription at Almack's is approved for this year." Leaning forward, she slid open a drawer in the small occasional table before her and removed a stack of pasteboard rectangles. "Three vouchers, for yourself, the Earl and the Lady Diana." She counted out three of the tickets and handed them to Lavinia, who gushed her thanks.

"Yes, yes." With an irritated wave of her hand, Sarah cut Lavinia off. "And here are yours, Ellen." She handed three more over.

"Three?" Marianne asked.

"One is yours, of course." Ellen pressed it into her hand.

"Oh… but I did not apply." She did not have the ten guineas for the subscription, or had not until that morning. She would have to visit Coutts again to pay Ellen back.

"I applied on your behalf. I could not possibly do without your company in my first full season trying to fit in with the Ton, Marianne. Besides, I shall quite depend on you to rein in Thomas' Americanisms, lest he offend someone unintentionally!"

Marianne smiled fondly at her friend. "I'm not sure Lord Havers is capable of offending anyone; he is far too nice!"

"Unless you mention the slave trade," Sarah remarked. "I rather thought he and Portland might come to blows when the topic came up at the Fulton dinner party! Portland was convinced he would be anti-emancipation, " she added to Marianne, who almost choked. She'd heard Thomas rage about the inhumanity of the slave trade on more than one occasion.

"Oh, please don't mention that again," Ellen begged. "I had rather hoped everyone forgot it."

"Quite the opposite. Castlereagh has spoken of it often with great admiration. I believe he is rather hoping Lord Havers will speak as eloquently on the topic in the House of Lords this year."

"Have no doubt of it." Ellen acknowledged Lady Jersey's approval.

Sarah nodded before reaching for a bell-pull beside her chair. "I shall have Frost fetch your other daughter, Lady Creighton. Pray excuse me; I am promised to a soiree at the Drummond-Burrells this evening."

"Thank you so much for your time, Lady Jersey." Taking her cue, Lavinia rose and offered a curtsey; Diana quickly followed suit. Ellen and Marianne made their farewells a little more leisurely, confident Lady Jersey's favour was not about to be withdrawn if they made the slightest misstep.

Clarissa met them in the entrance hall, taking her sister's arm and whispering to her. Diana still looked pale and nervous, but managed to respond to Clarissa's questioning with a small smile. Marianne was confident Diana would be fine, though it might take her some time to find her confidence among the London crowd. At least she had plenty of people looking out for her, unlike Marianne herself. There had been no one at all to speak for Marianne when her father had forced her

227

into a hasty marriage, nobody she might have run to for help.

What could anyone have done, anyway? Marianne mused as she sat opposite Ellen in the Havers carriage on their way home. She'd been eighteen and legally under her father's control. If Arthur decided to marry Diana off to some crony of his, there was little anyone could do about it legally. Outside the law - well, Marianne was quite certain she could smuggle herself and Diana onto a ship bound for the Americas, if it came to that. With her newfound wealth, opportunities presented which had never been open to her before.

"You look very thoughtful; what is on your mind?" Ellen asked from the other side of the carriage.

Marianne answered unthinkingly. "Running away to the Americas."

"Good God, not really?" Ellen looked shocked.

"Not really." Marianne gave her a reassuring smile. "Not for myself, at any rate, though should Diana find herself in an untenable situation due to Arthur or Lavinia's machinations, I would not hesitate to take her beyond their reach."

"Good for you," Ellen said. "I was in an untenable situation myself after my parents died and before Thomas took me in as part of the Havers family. Knowing there is a possible escape route would be a great comfort to any young woman, I think. I hope you will assure Diana, and Clarissa of course, that they may call upon Thomas and me as well as yourself should they need advice or assistance in anything."

"I shall, and thank you," Marianne said. "It's not that I think Arthur would do anything as terrible as what my father did to me, of course, but… well, Lavinia is very socially ambitious. I wouldn't put it past her to arrange a convenient compromise. I intend to take my chaperoning duties very seriously and attend every event to which they are invited."

"I will be right there beside you," Ellen promised. "It will be good practice, after all, for if I have daughters of my own one day!" Her hand slid to her stomach.

Marianne's eyes widened. "Are you expecting?" she gasped, excited for her friend.

"Perhaps." Ellen leaned close and lowered her voice, though they were quite alone. "I feel dreadfully queasy in the mornings. Susan has taken to bringing me tea and dry biscuits while I am still in bed, to stave off the nausea. I've made an appointment for the doctor to come tomorrow morning, while Thomas will be out. Will you attend me?"

"You haven't told him yet?"

"I want to wait until I am quite sure." Ellen looked down at her hands. "I quite understand if you don't want to. It must be a difficult subject for you."

It was at times like this she was forcibly recalled to the fact that while Ellen acted with remarkable maturity, the Countess of Havers was still only just turned one-and-twenty.

"I never, for one instant, wanted to bring a child into my marriage," Marianne stated with some force. Ellen stared at her wide-eyed, and she admitted, "Which does not mean, I never wanted a baby of my own."

Ellen didn't seem to know what to say, and Marianne was grateful the carriage halted just then outside the townhouse. It had been years since she'd dreamed of a child of her own, yet thinking of it now awakened feelings she had thought long dead. Unexpectedly, she found herself longing for a baby, a little boy perhaps with his father's dark hair and blue eyes.

When she realised she was imagining her son as Alexander's, she ran up the stairs as though chased by wolves, leaving a startled Ellen in her wake, hoping she hadn't upset her friend too badly.

Chapter Twenty

Brooks' Gentlemen's Club

"You'll never believe who I saw at Almack's yestereve," a loud voice announced behind Alexander, making him sigh and frown at his newspaper. He'd taken to spending afternoons at his club to escape the unending stream of guests visiting his mother, most of them accompanied by eligible daughters, sisters, nieces, or friends they hoped to throw at his head. He'd been rather enjoying the peace until the reading room was invaded by a couple of fools intent on rehashing their entire year to date, it seemed.

Now they had been joined by a third, even louder than the original two. Alexander was about to hush them when the newcomer spoke a name which froze him in place.

"Lady Creighton."

"What, the new one? Met her last week, she's got a daughter she's trying to fire off. Drab little thing."

"She has ten thousand, she's not so drab. Probably why the Patronesses gave them vouchers."

"Not the new one or her daughter, though they were both there too. I'm talking about the former one, whose given name is apparently Marianne. Marianne, Lady Creighton." The newcomer sighed it so dreamily Alexander couldn't quite help lowering his newspaper to see which silly youngster was mooning over Marianne.

His eyes widened with shock when he saw neither the newcomer nor the two he had joined were young; they were all men in their thirties, men for whom Alexander held at least some degree of respect. The one just slumping into a seat was Lord Ferry, second son of a duke and a wealthy man in his own right. Married, too, unless Alexander misremembered, but he was sure he'd met Lady Ferry at some event or other in the past year.

"She's more beautiful than ever," Lord Ferry continued. "And without that old fart Creighton around, she's smiling and dancing. I finally got that dance with her I've been begging years for."

Viscount Snowfield laughed, not unkindly. "Bit late now to make a play for her, ain't it? You've a wife and two brats at home."

"That's where you're wrong, my friend. The lady has been telling everyone who will listen she has no intention of marrying again." Ferry's smile was sly. "And you know what *that* means. She plans to be a merry widow."

Sir Edward Mullins, the third of the little party, sat up, suddenly paying attention. "Are you saying she'd accept a slip on the shoulder?"

"I think the lady knows her value and would be very expensive, but yes. I plan to offer her *carte blanche*." Ferry looked smug. "I know the way to her heart, I think. Her jewels all stayed with the Creighton coffers; she wore only a very plain little cross, whereas the new countess was wearing a spectacular diamond and ruby necklace. I'll buy her a diamond bracelet or two and set her up in a nice house wherever she wishes. Not many can match my resources."

"And most of those who can are as old as her first husband; I don't doubt she'll prefer someone who doesn't have one foot in the grave!" Snowfield laughed again, though Mullins looked a little disgruntled. "Well, I wish you luck in your pursuit, my friend. Will your wife object?"

"No, Honoria knows her place. She's breeding again, besides. I sent her back to stay with my parents."

Ferry's smile was so smug Alexander debated getting up just to punch it off his face. How *dare* the bastard talk about Marianne that way? How dare he even *think* it?

Starting a fight in the middle of Brooks' wouldn't help the situation, though. Alex briefly considered challenging Lord Ferry to defend Marianne's honour, but that would only fuel more gossip. All London would be saying that Marianne was already *Alex's* mistress within hours if he did challenge Ferry, which would do nobody any favours.

So instead of losing his temper, he folded his newspaper and laid it down on the table before getting up and leaving, offering a silent nod to the three men as he passed.

It wasn't a long walk to Cavendish Square, where the Havers had their townhouse. Alexander strode along briskly, temper simmering just below the surface. *I should have foreseen something like this happening*, he berated himself. He could not blame Marianne; she was only trying to protect herself, but in doing so she had accidentally opened herself to a far more iniquitous type of pursuit from gentlemen with less noble things on their minds than marriage.

"Good afternoon, Lord Glenkellie," the butler greeted him at the door. "Lord Havers is not at home this afternoon, I'm afraid."

"I was hoping to see Lady Havers and Lady Marianne, as it happens."

"Oh, they are but lately returned from shopping on Bond Street, my lord. I will see if Lady Havers will receive you, if you would care to wait?"

Alexander thrust his hat into the obliging man's hands. "Thank you, I will. If you wouldn't mind conveying that the matter is urgent?"

Ellen joined him in the parlour a few minutes later. "Glenkellie, what's so urgent?" she came straight to the point.

Glancing at the door, Alex wondered if he should wait for Marianne, but perhaps it was better she did not hear what he had to say.

"I need you to be very vigilant in keeping Lady Marianne by your side," he kept his voice low.

"Why?" Ellen asked in her usual straightforward way. "I am quite willing to do as you ask, but if there is anything in particular I should look for, I would prefer to know. Forewarned is forearmed."

"Quite so, Lady Havers." Trying to think how best to phrase the truth without being offensive, Alex said carefully, "It has come to my attention that Lady Marianne's public declaration that she does not intend to marry again may have given the wrong impression in certain quarters."

Ellen looked completely blank.

He sighed and tried again. "I overheard some gossip in my club regarding the possibility of Lady Marianne accepting a less than respectable offer."

This time, Ellen understood. Outrage dawned in her expression and she spluttered for a moment before saying, "Good God, some men really are just… just…"

"Horses' behinds?" Alex suggested.

"Exactly!"

"Who's a horse's behind?" Marianne asked as she entered the room.

Alex and Ellen looked at each other.

"If there is anyone specific you could name, I know I'd want to know so I could avoid them," Ellen said.

"Very well." Alex winced, but turned to Marianne. "You're acquainted with Lord Ferry, I understand?"

"Yes, for some years now." Marianne's brows drew down in a frown. "What about him?"

"I'm afraid your declaration that you do not intend to remarry has given Lord Ferry the wrong impression. His intentions towards you are less than honourable."

Dark colour rushed to Marianne's cheeks. "And you know this, how?" she asked after a moment of silence.

"He was gossiping about his intentions in Brooks'. I overheard," Alex said apologetically.

"*Damn* men!" The words exploded from Marianne, her fists clenching with anger as she turned to pace over to the window and glare out.

"If you would excuse me a moment," Ellen said, "I wish to let the staff know Lord Ferry is never to be admitted to this house under any pretext." She left the room, her heels clipping on the polished wooden floor.

In the silence, Alexander wondered if he should leave too, but Marianne was clearly overset. Not wanting to press her, he moved over to the window adjacent to where she stood and sat down on the cushioned window seat, thinking he would just keep her quiet company until Ellen returned. He was quite surprised when she turned from her contemplation of the street outside and sat down beside him.

"Have you ever discovered any disadvantages to being blessed with good looks?" Marianne asked unexpectedly.

Surprised, Alex shook his head. "No, but they are spoiled now." Unconsciously, he fingered the scar on his cheek. He'd already seen distaste from plenty of ladies as their eyes lingered on it.

"Nonsense, it only makes you look more distinguished," Marianne said with a sniff. "I wonder if it would work for me, though? Some sort of disfigurement - perhaps I could cut all my hair off."

"You would still be the most beautiful woman I know, even if you went ahead and did it," Alex answered, trying to concentrate on her words rather than the warm feelings engendered by her compliment.

Marianne eyed him, her expression wary. "You're not going to tell me I must not?"

"Why should I? 'Tis your hair. I would miss your crowning glory," daringly, he reached out to touch a curl which dangled along her neck, "but I have no right to tell you what to do. That is rather the point of you not wishing to marry again, isn't it?"

"Indeed, but there are plenty of men who would still try to tell me what I may or may not do, without any reason to claim authority over me whatsoever."

Alex offered her a sympathetic smile. "Perhaps you should use that as a tactic to weed out those you do not wish to associate with. Tell them you are considering cutting your hair off, and anyone who tries to tell you not to is not truly worthy of your friendship."

"I fear I should be left with only you and Havers as friends." Marianne's answering smile was wry.

"A tragic but honest assessment of my gender," Alex agreed ruefully.

They sat in silence for a moment before Marianne asked him another unexpected question. "If - *when* you take a wife, Glenkellie, would you forbid her to cut her hair off?"

"Certainly not," he said at once, then re-thought. "I might try to *persuade* her not to, but if she was quite set on it, I would ask that she let a maid do it, lest she injure herself with scissors when trying to cut at the back of her head where she cannot see."

Her expression was wistful. "That is an even better answer than your first response. Your wife will be a lucky woman."

"I hope she will think so," was the only response he could think of, aside from falling to his knees and begging her to marry him. It was definitely not the best moment for a proposal.

But dear God, if only he could!

Chapter Twenty-One

The Duchess of Balford's Ball

Marianne was still angry by the time she arrived at the Balford ball. Determined to stand firm in the face of spiteful gossip, she had taken particular care with her appearance, selecting one of her most beautiful gowns, a silk creation which changed between blue and green depending on the light. Simple in cut, it depended entirely on the quality of the fabric and the beauty of the wearer to carry it off. She knew she'd achieved the desired effect when Lavinia took one look at her and sighed in despair.

"Nobody will even look at Diana, with you here," she said dismally.

"Lavinia." Marianne shook her head. "You do not *want* a man for Diana whose head might be turned by me. Such a man would not suit her at all, and you do want her to be happy, don't you?"

Obviously struck by the argument, Lavinia nodded in agreement. "I daresay you are correct," she conceded.

"And look, here is the Marquis of Glenkellie to claim you for the first dance," Marianne told Diana, who was looking very pretty in a white gown with a silver net overlay, tiny silver stars sparkling in her dark brown hair. "Everyone will be asking who the lovely young lady he could hardly wait to dance with is, believe me."

Diana smiled shyly back at her. "I know he would far rather be dancing with you," she whispered as Lavinia turned away for a moment to speak to an acquaintance.

"Well, to tell the truth, there isn't anyone else I should like to dance with," Marianne admitted. Ever since Alexander had revealed the gossip to her and Ellen yesterday, she had been thinking about it; if Lord Ferry, a married man, was looking at her with speculation, who could she possibly trust? She would look at every dance partner with caution from now on.

Alexander arrived before them and executed a bow to each of them, greeting them very politely.

"I hope you have not given away my dance, Lady Diana?" he said with a warm twinkle. "The musicians are tuning up now, and I believe we will open with a quadrille."

"The quadrille is quite my favourite," Diana said shyly, placing her hand on his proffered arm. "I am very sensible of the honour you do me, Lord Glenkellie; thank you for asking me to dance."

"It is I who am honoured, Lady Diana." His eyes crinkled at the corners. "That is, so long as you do not step on my toes!"

Diana giggled as Alexander led her away, and Lavinia shook her head. "He's not remotely interested in her, I think, but he does seem very nice."

"Quite the nicest man of my acquaintance," Marianne said a little wistfully.

"Lavinia, who's that tall chap dancing with Diana?" Arthur hurried up to them, rather out of breath. He didn't bother to greet Marianne.

"The Marquis of Glenkellie, dear. You recall, Marianne introduced us to him and the dowager marchioness at the theatre last week, and he requested a dance with Diana."

"A marquis," Arthur puffed up. "Well, that's a coup! Glenkellie's very rich, I hear."

"Do not get your hopes up." Lavinia shook her head. "He only asked as a favour to Marianne, I think."

"Why should he owe *you* favours?"

Arthur looks rather like a carp, Marianne thought, his eyes bulging and his mouth open as he turned to her.

"Lord Glenkellie owes me nothing," she said, "but we are old friends."

"Indeed!" Arthur's brows shot up, and then he leaned forward. "You may have made a cuckold out of my uncle," he said viciously, "but you're still a Creighton, and I'll not have you bringing the name into disrepute. There are already rumours circulating about you!"

"Arthur!" Lavinia sounded genuinely shocked. Grasping her husband's arm, she shot Marianne an apologetic look. "Pray excuse us."

Marianne was more than happy to turn on her heel and hurry away. *How could anyone ever believe she had cuckolded her husband?* He had never tolerated her so much as *speaking* to another man unless he was present, had punished *her* if gentlemen tried to approach, claiming she must have enticed them with her smile, her manner. She would not have the slightest idea *how* to encourage a suitor!

Blinded by tears of rage and hurt, Marianne pushed her way through the crowd, finally escaping the ballroom and hurrying to a retiring room.

Alexander witnessed Marianne's flight and Lady Havers going in hasty pursuit. Caught in the middle of the dance floor, he could only bite his lip and watch, hoping Ellen could help with whatever had obviously upset Marianne.

"Are you in love with my aunt?"

The blunt question from Lady Diana as the pattern of the dance brought them back together made him miss a step.

"I beg your pardon?" he stuttered.

"Because I think she's in love with you." Diana's brown eyes were clear and guileless as she looked up at him.

"She claims she doesn't want to marry."

"She doesn't want to marry someone who would treat her as appallingly as my great-uncle did, she means. Would you treat her badly?"

"I would treat her like a queen," Alexander said, heartfelt.

Diana smiled. "I thought so. Your eyes give you away when you see her, you know."

"And to think, I thought you were shy," he marvelled.

"I am, rather." She blushed prettily. "But sometimes, direct action is called for, and I can be brave if I must. Clarissa and I talked and she said I absolutely had to talk to you. Especially since Mama thinks, er..." she trailed off.

"Thinks I should marry you?" Alexander asked.

"Well, yes. I should never want a husband in love with someone else, though, so I should take it as a very great favour if you do *not* pay me too much attention."

"Noted," he said gravely. "And thank you."

"What for?"

"Helping me come to a decision I have been pondering for some time: what exactly I should say to Lady Marianne. You are correct that I am in love with her, and marrying someone else wouldn't be fair to anyone involved."

Diana is really quite beautiful when she smiles like that, Alexander thought as the dance ended and everyone applauded the musicians. Offering his arm, he led Diana back to her mother and thanked her for the dance. Young men were already flocking around, jostling for introductions, and he paused to say to Diana, quietly so that nobody else would overhear, "Should you ever require any assistance, I pray you will not hesitate to call upon me."

"Thank you, Lord Glenkellie." She sank into a curtsey. "I am sure your partner for the next dance is eagerly awaiting you."

He hoped so. With a final bow in the Countess' direction, he turned and headed for the ballroom doors, hoping Marianne might have returned to the room. He could not see her or Ellen Havers anywhere.

Lady Jersey was close by the door, and he paused to offer his respects and ask whether she had seen Marianne. "She promised me the second dance," he said, trying to make his voice sound casual. "I've waited almost a decade to dance with her, you know."

"I do know, as a matter of fact. Not just a dance you've been waiting for either, is it?" Lady Jersey's eyes were uncomfortably sharp. "Don't waste any more time, Glenkellie."

"I'm trying, my lady."

"She's skittish, and rightfully so, but I believe she trusts you. Don't let her down."

"I won't."

Behind Lady Jersey, Alex saw Marianne re-entering the ballroom, Lady Havers by her side. Her colour was a little high, but she was holding her chin up defiantly, her green eyes flashing fire.

Alex approached quickly, making a low bow. "Lady Marianne," he said. "The second dance is about to begin, if you are still willing to grant me the honour?"

She hesitated, and then said, "Would you mind if we danced the third instead of this one? I would like a little fresh air."

The French doors leading to the terrace were thrown wide open to allow cool air into the room, so Alex led her in that direction. Outside, he was careful to lead her to the balustrade well in view of everyone in the ballroom, so nobody could say any impropriety might be occurring.

"I saw you leave the room in something of a hurry a little while ago. Did your nephew say something to upset you?" Alex asked, trying to be tactful. He wanted to demand answers -- maybe punch Arthur a few times for putting that look on her face -- but he had no right to demand anything from Marianne.

"He seems to manage it on a regular basis," Marianne said, her mouth twisting as though she tasted something bad. "Pray, do not concern yourself."

"But I do concern myself," Alex let a little of the intense emotion he felt spill over into his words, "I find myself very concerned for you, Marianne. If gossip has reached your nephew, he could make your life very uncomfortable."

Her face tightened a little, but she met his eyes steadily. "I hope my friends know who I truly am... Alexander."

"I know who you are. You are not only the most beautiful woman I know, you are also the bravest person I've ever met, man *or* woman."

Startled at his description of her, Marianne blinked. "I'm not brave."

"How can you say that? You survived a living hell of a marriage for eight years, never letting anyone else know your true feelings. You carry scars to the soul as deep as any soldier, and yet you concern yourself more with the happiness of others than your soul. Your courage both awes and humbles me."

They stood a decorous foot apart, staring at each other, yet Marianne felt almost as though he enfolded her in a warm, comforting embrace. There was no doubting the sincerity of Alexander's words... or the depth of his regard for her.

"I cannot bear to see you insulted and degraded," he said at last, when she could not find words to speak. "I cannot. I know you do not wish to marry, and I would never press you, though my heart's desire is… well, I said I would not, and I will not." His jaw clenched as though he was struggling with himself, and she saw his fists were opening and closing at his sides. "Instead, I wish to offer you something else, with no expectations. My mother plans to travel to Italy to visit with her sister this year; she will remain at least a twelvemonth. She has taken a liking to you and pressed me to ask if you would like to accompany her."

Marianne's mouth fell open. "Your mother wants me to go to Italy with her?" she said at last, incredulously.

"Indeed. My aunt is widowed and lives in Florence; she is a *duchessa* and very well respected. You might wish to remain with her there, if you wish."

"Because here, there will always be gossip and innuendo," Marianne said quietly. "You're offering me an *escape*."

Her hand rested on the stone balustrade at the edge of the terrace, and he reached out to put his own over it. "I would offer you everything I have, everything I am, if only you would accept," Alexander said.

She could see it in his eyes, his love as intense and unchanging as the day he had been forced to leave her to go to war. "I promised I'd wait for you, and I couldn't," she whispered.

"I promised I would come back for you, and I failed you. I can never make up for what you suffered, but please, Marianne. Allow me to be of service, in this or any other way you wish."

His fingers were warm on hers, and she wanted more. Wanted his arms around her, wanted the *safety* of him, the sure and certain knowledge that he sought only to make her happy.

"Ask me." She could barely get the words out, her voice a thin croak, and she had to repeat herself before Alexander's eyes widened in comprehension.

Slowly, he lifted her hand and brought it to his lips, his eyes never leaving hers.

"Lady Marianne," he said, and she loved him all the more for his choice to be formal while avoiding the hated name of Creighton, "would you do me the very great honour of granting me your hand in marriage?"

She had to take a deep breath to answer, but he had called her the bravest person she knew, and his belief in her courage made it easier to believe in herself.

"Only if you promise we can go to Italy on our honeymoon. I've always wanted to see Florence."

Chapter Twenty-Two

Alexander could hardly believe what he was hearing as Marianne spoke, her words making all his dreams come true. "Anything," he promised fervently. "Anywhere you wish."

"Only, perhaps we could wait until later in the year? I did promise to go to Amelia Pembroke when she is brought to bed with her child, and I think Ellen Havers may need me in August for the same reason." Marianne gave him an appealing look, one he knew he would always struggle to resist.

"Wait until August to get married?" Alexander's distress at the thought of waiting so long must have been quite obvious, because Marianne chuckled and squeezed his fingers gently between her gloved ones.

Catherine Bilson

"No, no. Just to go to Italy. I should like to get married as soon as it can be arranged, actually. I think we have waited quite long enough."

"Far too long," he agreed, lifting her hand to kiss it again. A loud cough nearby recalled him to their situation and the distinct lack of privacy, and he lowered her hand with a grimace.

"This is a poor time and place for this conversation, but I hope you will allow me to say that you have made me the happiest man in England."

"Perhaps you might call for me tomorrow and you can tell me then," Marianne teased him.

"A drive in Hyde Park?" Alexander suggested, and she inclined her head in acceptance.

"So long as you remember to bring the bread."

"Oh, I will not forget, I promise. I cannot ever recall seeing you so happy as when you fed the ducks the other day!" Her laughter had been a balm to his wounded soul; he had sent his driver to get more bread so they might stay longer. If Marianne wanted to hand-feed every duck on London on a daily basis, he would buy a bakery to provide her with an endless supply of bread.

Marianne giggled, her eyes bright with mischief. "I can only think of one other time I *have* ever been so happy, Alexander… and that is right at this very moment."

"You have truly made me the happiest man in the world," he said through a thick lump of emotion in his throat. "I can only strive in every way I can conceive of to give you equal joy in return."

They returned to the ballroom in time for the third dance. Alexander felt lighter than he had in many years as they moved together through the patterns of the dance, Marianne's happy countenance buoying his spirits. Spotting his mother standing near the edge of the dance floor, he sent her a joyous grin. This was not the appropriate venue to announce their engagement, but tomorrow he would send a notice to the newspapers and perhaps his mother would host a dinner party in the next week or so.

Since Marianne was a widow, there was nobody Alex need apply to for her hand, though he supposed he should do her nephew the courtesy of advising him privately of their engagement. Perhaps he'd stop by the Creighton townhouse after he returned Marianne home tomorrow.

"September would be a good time to leave for Italy," he remarked to Marianne as the dance brought them together. "The seas will not be too rough then, and winter is much milder in the southern climes. We could spend much of the summer at Glenkellie if you like, before going to Havers Hall in August, and then taking ship once you are happy to leave Lady Havers."

"I think that sounds a wonderful plan," Marianne agreed. "Shall we see Rome as well as Florence?"

"Indeed, and Venice too, and anywhere else you might wish. Do you wish to see only Italy, or have you a hankering to visit other places in the Mediterranean?"

"You truly will take me anywhere I wish to go, won't you?" Marianne said in wondering tones as the dance ended.

Alexander offered his arm to lead her from the floor. "Of course I will. Anything you wish for, you need only name it. The throne of England might be slightly beyond my resources, but any lesser goal, I will do anything within my power to attain for you."

"Now just a minute," a loud voice interrupted, and Alex looked around to see Lord Ferry scowling pugnaciously at him. "Are you trying to cut me out, Glenkellie? Damn it, I knew you overheard in Brooks'. Lady Creighton," he turned to Marianne, "I can assure you, my resources are beyond anything Glenkellie can muster from his Scottish hillsides. You may name your price."

Gasps of shock rippled around them, and Alex tensed. *What the hell was Ferry thinking?* He'd just propositioned Marianne in *public*!

"Lord Ferry," Marianne said in a very clear, cold voice, "I am not for sale at *any* price."

"Come now…" Ferry blustered.

But Alex had heard more than enough. "Ferry," he said, in a low, dangerous voice, "you are speaking to the future Marchioness of Glenkellie. You may apologise now, or you'll meet me at dawn."

Ferry froze, mouth wide open as he took in Alexander's murderous expression, before he gulped audibly. "I, ah," he said, "Ah, ah, do beg your pardon, Glenkellie."

"Not apologise to *me*," Alexander said in disgust, "to the *lady*." God, the man was a complete craven. It would have been satisfying as hell to run him through for the insult. Instead, he had to stand and watch Ferry's panicked, fawning apology to a tight-lipped Marianne.

"Go away, you repulsive little man," Marianne said at last, and everyone with earshot, all of whom had been hanging on every word of the confrontation, burst out laughing.

Crimson-faced, Lord Ferry fled.

"His *poor* wife," Marianne said with a sigh, turning back to Alex. He was fighting down his own laughter and couldn't speak.

"Well done, dearest," another voice said, and Alex turned to see his mother approaching. She drew Marianne into a fond embrace. "What a marchioness you will be! You must let me introduce you to my very dear friend, the Duchess of Balford. Alexander? Do get us some champagne, there's a dear." She pressed an empty glass into his hand and drew Marianne away into a crowd of elegantly dressed ladies.

Alexander could hardly get near Marianne for the rest of the ball. Ladies who had twitched their skirts aside earlier in the evening fawned over her now, and word spread fast of her magnificent set-down of Lord Ferry... faster than news of their engagement, as they were soon to discover.

"A high-perch phaeton!" Marianne clapped her hands with glee as she descended the steps of the Havers townhouse on Alexander's arm the following morning. "I have always wanted to ride in one of these!"

"I know. You mentioned it once to me, long ago. I said one day I would have one and take you driving in it, do you remember?"

"I do, though I had not thought on it until this moment. I'm surprised *you* remember!" She turned luminous eyes up to him as he handed her carefully up into the seat and accepted the reins from his tiger.

"The dream of riding with you proudly sitting at my side kept me going through some of the darkest times during the war," he said quietly, drawing a thick blanket placed on the seat over her lap and tucking it in to keep her warm.

Laying one hand on his arm, Marianne tilted her head deliberately to show off her pretty hat and said, "Then let us to Hyde Park, my lord. You shall have your fill of riding with me today. We might even need to stop for fresh horses!"

Alex's laugh lingered behind them as the horses set off at a brisk trot.

Talking and laughing and having to stop every few minutes to greet someone who wished to congratulate them, they had been parading through Hyde Park for over an hour when Marianne spied her family. "Look, in that open landau there! We must stop, Alexander."

261

Lavinia was smiling, Diana beside her waving excitedly until her mother placed a gentle restraining hand on her arm. Marianne smiled back. She and Lavinia would never be close, but at least she was reasonably confident Lavinia wouldn't try to force any of her daughters into marriages they did not want. Hopefully she would check the worst of Arthur's ambitions and be an advocate for her daughters if they needed it.

Arthur did not look pleased to see them. "A word, Glenkellie?" he said crisply once polite greetings had been exchanged.

"Since I suspect this concerns you, would you care to accompany me?" Alexander asked Marianne. "I will gladly deal with it if you would rather not."

"I think I would prefer to be involved in discussions about my own future," Marianne decided. "Pray excuse me."

"Go home," Arthur instructed Lavinia. "I will walk back; it's not far."

Lavinia looked at Marianne, her expression concerned, but Marianne gestured she should go. After all, what could Arthur do to her with Alexander present? She was quite safe.

They left Alexander's tiger holding the horses and followed Arthur across the grass towards the

Serpentine, a glassy, reflective silver under the winter-grey sky. A pair of mute swans floated serenely by, a stark contrast to the churning in Marianne's stomach. Even though she tried to tell herself Arthur had no power over her, the prospect of a confrontation brought back old terrors.

Alexander's arm under her hand was strong and rock-steady; she drew strength from his calm assurance. *This was her choice*, she reminded herself. She didn't want to let Alexander handle all her problems, though she was confident he could do so. She was taking control of her own life and doing what she wanted, with his support.

Finally Arthur seemed to judge they were far enough from others to speak privately, and he whirled to face them. "What in God's name were you *thinking*?" he half-shouted. "A confrontation in the middle of a Society ball over *her*?"

Marianne blinked.

Alexander looked startled. "I beg your pardon?" he snapped, not sounding apologetic in the least. "Would you have me allow Lady Marianne's good name to be publicly sullied by a disrespectful arse of a man? Not while I breathe."

Arthur didn't even seem to hear him, puffed up with his own rage. "And you!" Turning on Marianne, he jabbed a finger at her. "Two

263

paramours almost coming to blows over you, in public! You *whore*!" Spittle flew as he shouted, and she instinctively took several steps back. Arthur looked only too much like his uncle, her dead husband, in one of his rages.

Alexander moved in front of her at once, letting out a sound a great deal like a snarl, but salvation came suddenly from a far less likely source.

One of the swans which a moment earlier was floating so peacefully on the water obviously took exception to Arthur's threatening gestures and shouts. In a swirling storm of white wings and enraged hissing, the swan attacked, thrashing at Arthur's face with beak and wings.

Cursing as he tried to beat the swan back, Arthur stumbled backwards, toppling into the shallow water behind him with a gigantic splash and a high-pitched shriek.

"Well," Alexander said with a deep chuckle as the swan continued to harass Arthur, "that saves me from planting him a facer, I suppose. Do you think your friends the ducks set that swan on him on purpose?"

Marianne could not hold it in; she burst out laughing, a release of tension like a spring uncoiling inside her bubbling up and out of her mouth in throaty giggles. She could only lean on Alexander and watch as her nephew received a thorough thrashing, quite at the mercy of the furious bird.

The swan finally backed off, retreating to guard its mate, still hissing in Arthur's direction occasionally as the Earl of Creighton climbed out of the water, sobbing with rage and cradling one hand close to his chest in obvious pain.

"If you ever again speak to, or about, my future wife in any kind of derogatory way, I will kill you," Alexander said, his tone cold and dispassionate. "It is only for the sake of your wife and children that I allow the punishment God's creature has meted out to be satisfactory. Let this divine retribution be your final warning!"

They walked away with Marianne still laughing, hoping she would never forget the image of the dripping, spluttering Earl of Creighton casting fearful glances in equal measure at Alexander and the swan.

"Divine retribution indeed," she managed to splutter at last, as they returned to the phaeton and Alexander lifted her carefully up to the seat. "That was *wonderful*!"

"Perhaps we should foster a rumour that God will wreak vengeance on any who offend you." Alexander cast her a teasing grin as he took up the reins. "I daresay it would save both of us a great deal of trouble!"

In the distance, Arthur Creighton began the slow, soggy trudge across the grass away from the Serpentine, moaning at the pain in his injured hand and still keeping a wary eye on the swan.

The sun broke through the clouds just then, thin rays of bright yellow sunshine streaming down on the phaeton as the horses set off once again in a prancing trot. Marianne turned her face upwards, smiling as she thought that not so long ago, she would not have dared for fear of a freckle appearing on her nose. Alexander would likely tell her any emerging freckles were his favourite thing about her, because they were gained while she was enjoying herself. Snuggling closer to him under the thick blanket he tucked over both their laps, she rested her head against his shoulder and sighed with utter contentment.

Epilogue

Four weeks later
St. George's Church, Hanover Square

Alexander's heart was full as he watched Marianne walk towards him, wearing a stunning new gown of pale gold silk trimmed with white Brussels lace. While Arthur had issued a suitably grovelling apology the day after the swan incident in Hyde Park, Marianne had declined his offer to walk her down the aisle. Instead, she walked alone, preceded by her youngest niece Penelope, strewing freshly picked snowdrops in her path.

He'd offered to denude every hothouse in London for more expensive flowers for her, of course, but Marianne had told him she'd far rather have snowdrops, that earliest of spring blooms, easily gathered in February.

"The are the first flowers of spring, the season of new beginnings," she'd told him, and Alexander at once had agreed there could be no flower more appropriate.

While he had hoped to obtain a special licence and wed Marianne within a week of her acceptance, his mother and Marianne had persuaded him that waiting for the banns to be called and throwing a grand wedding with the cream of the Ton on the guest list would forever silence any gossip.

Since he was entirely at Marianne's mercy, he'd agreed to whatever they wanted, though he'd privately bemoaned to her his reluctance to wait even a day more than he had to for her.

"We've waited this long," she'd told him tenderly, placing her soft hand against his cheek. "I want - no, I *need* - this wedding to be as different from my first as it is possible to be, Alexander."

Understanding, he'd kicked himself for his insensitivity. "Only tell me what I need do to make it so, beloved."

"Be patient with me - and be yourself," she'd told him, reaching up to kiss him lovingly.

Marianne's hand trembled a little in her white silk glove as she placed it in Alexander's, and he looked a query at her, brow furrowing with concern. She smiled back at him determinedly. The ghosts of her past were not going to cloud this, the wedding day she'd always wanted.

Instead of her father and two bored servants as witnesses in a dusty parlour, there was a church filled with her and Alexander's friends and family. The vicar was a kindly, serious gentleman who had insisted on speaking to them both privately before the ceremony, intent on being certain they were both happy before proceeding. And last but certainly not least, instead of a leering old man, there was her beloved Alexander, tall and handsome, his eyes filled with love for her as he spoke his vows.

"Yes," she said it loud and clear as the vicar asked if she accepted Alexander as her husband. "I do."

His smile was filled with both joy and relief as he squeezed her hands, and Marianne gazed lovingly back at him as the ceremony concluded and they emerged from the church to the rousing cheers of their friends.

Thomas and Ellen Havers had insisted on throwing a wedding party for them after the ceremony, and afterwards they planned to return to Alexander's townhouse and remain in London for another month before travelling to Hampshire to visit with the Pembrokes -- the only friends who were unable to attend their wedding. Too close to her confinement, Amelia had instead sent many excited letters and a promise of a gentle mare from their famous stables as a wedding gift for Marianne.

Once Amelia's child was born, they would go to Portsmouth and take ship there for Scotland, cutting several days off the journey to Glenkellie. Marianne was looking forward very much to seeing Alexander's childhood home, which he described as 'an ancient pile' but his mother had told her was one of the most beautiful castles in Scotland.

Lady Helena was sailing for Italy in late March, and they would join her in September after Marianne saw Ellen through her confinement as well. She had already cornered Lavinia, who as the mother of five children was the most experienced source on childbirth she knew, and quizzed her for so much detail Lavinia turned quite pale.

Their conversations had taught Marianne about a great deal more than just childbirth, however. Despite a great deal of blushing, Lavinia had imparted quite a lot of knowledge about what happened in the marriage bed when the wife wasn't unwilling.

Knowing happy couples like the Havers and the Pembrokes, Marianne had slowly become aware there could be true and genuine affection between husband and wife. More than once while staying with Thomas and Ellen she had accidentally come across them in a passionate embrace, and the thought of sharing such embraces with Alexander made her feel quite warm and flushed.

Far from fearing her second wedding night, she was rather looking forward to it.

"Do you think anyone would notice if we sneaked away?" she whispered to Alexander after they had dined and danced and talked for what felt like hours.

"To go where? Are you feeling quite well?" He looked at her with concern.

"Oh, I'm fine." Sliding her hand into his, she squeezed. "I would like to be alone with my husband, that's all."

"Really?" A wide grin broke across his face. "Then let us not waste another minute, my darling marchioness!"

They slipped out and ran down the stairs, jumping into the waiting Glenkellie coach, where

Alexander lost no time pulling Marianne into his arms.

"I love you," he whispered, raining kisses across her face. "I have always, always loved you."

"I love you, too," Marianne said, nestling close against him and resting her head against his strong shoulder, safe in his arms and secure in the knowledge that she was finally right where she had always longed to be.

~ THE END ~

A Note From The Author

A Marquis For Marianne is the second book in the Blushing Brides series. If you haven't already read *An Earl For Ellen* and discovered Thomas and Ellen Havers' love story, do go and grab it now!

The next book in the series will be *A Duke For Diana*, where Marianne's shy niece Diana finds her feet and her own path when she and her sister Clarissa are invited to join their aunt on her wedding trip to Italy!

I hope you enjoyed reading *A Marquis For Marianne*. If you did, I hope you will consider leaving a review of the book on Amazon or Goodreads, so that other potential readers can see your recommendation!

With thanks and best wishes
Catherine Bilson
Brisbane, Australia
March 2019